Pet Shop Passion

SAMANTHA MICHAELS

Created with Vellum

Thank you to my husband and our dog for putting up with me! Thank you to my friends and family for their support. Thanks to the other authors I've connected with for being such an inspiration. Thank you to my awesome PA Zoe for all her support. Special thanks to the readers for supporting my books!! You're why I keep doing this!!

Chapter One

Bang!

He heard the door slam, followed by the clicking of heels, and he sighed audibly. His afternoon of peace and quiet was over.

"Mikael," Liza shouted.

Mikael Alfredsson, kick-ass rock bassist, sat quietly in his office, trying to buy himself a few more minutes of solitude. Mikael had become a shell of his former self since Liza came into his life. He came to America as a teenager, having been born and raised in Sweden. He had a naughty sense of humor, especially when it came to his love of role-playing in the bedroom. That combined with his rugged good looks, women had always fallen at his feet and he loved every minute of it. Now, he was the errand boy and ATM machine for the vicious she-devil that was stomping her way to his office. Mikael was never one of those musicians who made millions, but he did earn enough to live comfortably, at least until Liza came along. She came from money, being the only daughter of a prominent record company owner, the very record company that had signed Mikael's band.

The wealth she had from the trust fund her father gave her wasn't enough for her and she quickly latched on to Mikael, never being shy about spending as much of his money as she could get her hands on. He had a decent amount he kept hidden from her in case he ever did get the chance to escape her clutches. Despite her nasty attitude and the way she treated him, she had this hold on him and he just couldn't seem to break himself free. Who am I trying to kid, he thought, I know exactly why. There were days where he'd had enough of her, but he knew that kicking her to the curb wasn't an option. She had made that clear when they first got together. They were out to dinner and Liza was being horrible to their waiter.

"You were extremely rude to our waiter. All he did was ask what you wanted to drink."

"He looked at me," she huffed.

"Because he was speaking to you!'

"He's a lowly waiter, he should NOT be looking at me."

"Oh, for fuck's sake, you're a person, just like he is." Actually, better, Mikael thought to himself.

"Yeah, no, he's beneath us."

"No, he isn't. I was a waiter prior to signing my first record deal. I'm no better a person today than I was then. I just do something different for a living."

"Whatever."

"I'm not going to continue dating you if you don't start treating people better."

"You'll never leave me," she sneered.

"Don't be so sure."

"Trust me. You do and I go running right to daddy."

"Big fuckin' deal."

"It is a big deal. I tell daddy I'm unhappy and your contract dissolves."

It was at that moment Mikael knew he was stuck in this hell for as long as she wanted. He needed the income from his record deal, so he had to give in to her every whim. She took plenty but rarely gave in return, especially in the bedroom. Even sex was always on her terms, leaving him more often than not full of pent up sexual desire. If ever he got to the point that he no longer needed that record deal, she would be history. Hell, she wasn't even his type.

Mikael always had a thing for curvy brunettes, especially when those women were confident and sexually experienced. Nothing was sexier than a woman who knew what she wanted in bed, or anywhere else she was willing to fuck. His reverie was broken by her screechy voice invading the silence of his office, causing his cat, Leo, to run off.

"Why didn't you answer me?" she demanded.

"Didn't hear you."

"What-ever. What's on that paper?"

"Just got off the phone with Dean. He's gettin' hitched, so I was checkin' flights."

"Tell me it's not to that hellhole he moved to."

"It's a great area from what he told me."

"How long?"

"Just a few days, for the bachelor party, rehearsal dinner and the wedding."

"Nope."

"Excuse me?"

"I don't wanna go."

"I don't fuckin' care. Dean's my friend."

"What If I refuse?"

"I'm going whether you do or not."

"Fine, but I'm only coming to the wedding."

"What-ever," he mocked.

"Keep it up and I call daddy."

Before he could respond, she turned on her stilettos and stormed out. He gave her the finger behind her back, which gave him a tiny bit of satisfaction, though he knew it would be gone the next time they were in the same room. He didn't tell her that after talking to Dean and hearing how great his life was now, he wanted that too. Maybe life far away from LA and the music business was also what he needed. No time to think about that now, as he heard his name being screamed yet again.

He walked out to the kitchen to see what all the damn yelling was about.

"What's wrong?"

"I want water NOW."

"You're standing right next to the fridge."

"And?"

"For fuck's sake."

Mikael grabbed a bottle of water and put it down on the counter next to here. Without so much as a nod, she turned and stomped off, earning her another middle finger. He walked back to his office and found Leo curled up on his desk. Absentmindedly petting him, he called his travel agent to book their flights. Luckily for him, Liza's reputation preceded her, so his agent didn't question why they were flying on separate days. He also took care of the hotel. He purposely picked the hotel with the least amenities just to piss Liza off. The wedding was only a month away, and he couldn't wait, mostly to have a couple days without that nag up his ass.

Not wanting to face her any more that night, he ended up sleeping on the couch in his office with Leo curled up next to him. His restful night's sleep was interrupted much too early when the she-devil woke up and was demanding breakfast that she damn well could have gotten herself. He walked out to the kitchen and saw her sitting at the table with her arms folded.

"Where the hell's my breakfast?"

"Did you make it?"

"NO! I don't cook."

"Then go out and get something."

"I'll call daddy."

"Fine. What do you want?"

"Egg white omelet."

Mikael didn't say a word and just made her breakfast. He would give anything to be with someone who would do things for him once in a while. Maybe it was time just to send her packing. If only that was an option. After he served her highness breakfast, he headed to his office at the studio where he could be left alone. He was working on recording some bass tracks for an upcoming project and spent as much time there as he could. He liked when she was already asleep by the time he got home. He would always just sleep in his home office so he didn't wake her.

After he finished what he wanted to get done that day, he was just sitting thinking about how disillusioned he'd become with the whole LA scene. He'd been in the music business for close to 30 years and was starting to get burnt out. He started thinking again about his friend and how much the change of scenery had improved his life and Mikael found himself wanting the same. Luckily for him, the next month went by fairly quickly and it was time to head East for the wedding.

He had a mid-morning flight so he had packed the night before. He got up early to head to the airport, allowing ample time to get through security. He was actually glad Liza wasn't flying with him as she was a royal pain in the ass, very demanding to the flight attendants and rude to other passengers. He would be much happier flying with his friends and their wives. He was sitting in the waiting area when he saw the rest of the group coming through security.

"No Liza?" Andy asked.

"Didn't wanna come this early. She's coming in the day of the rehearsal dinner."

"Sorry, man."

"It's okay, at least I don't have to listen to her mouth."

Everyone laughed. They all felt for Mikael, especially knowing he was stuck with her as long as he wanted to keep his contract. Andy and their other friend Damon were grateful they had the amazing wives they had and really wished Mikael could find the same thing.

"Maybe you'll meet someone at the wedding," Damon chimed in.

Mikael smiled but he didn't say anything. If only he could meet someone like Dean's fiancee, Alex. The way Dean talked about her, she sounded like the type of woman Mikael wished he was with. Even if he did meet someone, what would it matter? He sighed loudly, that familiar feeling of being trapped washing over him and sending him into a lousy mood. A little while later, they heard their boarding announcement, so they headed over to the counter to show their boarding passes and head to their seats. Once boarding was complete, they took off and several hours later, they touched down in Philadelphia.

They rented a van so they could all ride together to the hotel. The plan was to shower and change then head over to the night club where the bachelor/bachelorette party was being held. When they arrived, the other guests were already there and everyone introduced themselves to each other while they waited for the guests of honor. Mikael noticed that one of Alex's friends was alone. He had to admit, he took an instant liking to her. She was exactly the type of woman that he preferred.

Mikael found out her name was Hannah Davidson and that she owned the hottest pet supply store in their town, 'Rock the Fur.' Hannah was average height, but that was the only thing average about her. She was curvy in all the right places. Her long brown hair cascaded halfway down her back and she had the most beautiful green eyes he'd ever seen. He also found out she was a bit clumsy when she dropped an open sugar packet down her dress.

He felt something stirring inside his gut that had been dormant since he started seeing Liza. He couldn't seem to take his eyes off her. When the guests of honor arrived, the women went next door for a couple hours while the men stayed here. The whole time the stripper danced, all Mikael could think about was seeing Hannah naked. After their separate parties, the group came back together for dancing. Mikael walked over to Hannah, who was sitting by herself sipping coffee and watching the other couples enjoy themselves.

"Would you like to dance, Sugartits?"

"Excuse me, what the hell did you just call me?"

"Sugartits. Kinda saw what happened with the sugar packet."

"Damn, I was hoping nobody noticed, Pepperballs."

Mikael laughed so loudly, everyone stopped and stared at him.

"Now, about that dance?"

"Me? But you're a rock star."

"And?"

"I'm just a nobody."

"You're certainly not a nobody. Come on."

"Um, I guess."

Mikael put his hand out and helped Hannah up then walked her to dance floor. She felt electricity course through her veins at just that small tough. He put his arms around her and pulled her close, as she circled her arms around his neck. She fit his body perfectly and he felt his heart start racing. They swayed together slowly to the music. The feeling of her body against his was intoxicating, and he desperately wanted to kiss her. He almost did, until Liza's face floated through his head.

The party went on for several more hours and they danced for the rest of the night. He loved being with someone who was enjoying herself, not sitting in judgment of everyone with a sour look on her face. Liza never danced for fear she might get a drop of sweat on her face. Hannah on the other hand didn't care that she was sweaty and that her hair was matted to her face.

"Can we meet somewhere after the party?" Mikael asked.

"Why?"

"To get to know each other."

"But you have a girlfriend."

"So what. I'm just talking about grabbing some coffee, not having sex."

Hannah felt a sensation run through her body straight to that magical place between her legs. "I really don't think it's a good idea."

"Why not? I won't bite. I mean, unless you want me too."

There went that sensation again. "Just coffee?"

"Scout's honor."

"I guess it's alright."

Mikael's face lit up. "Can you pick me up? We all rode here together."

"I'm still not sure this is a good idea."

"I promise I won't try anything."

"It's not that. What if your girlfriend finds out?"

"She won't. Nobody else likes her."

"Oh."

"So, can you pick me up?"

"What hotel?"

"The Inn at Leola Village."

"I know where that is."

"Park in a far corner and I'll come back down once everyone's in their rooms."

"Okay."

Hannah followed their van to the hotel and pulled off to the side until she saw everyone go into their rooms. Mikael came back out, walked over to her car, and got in. Hannah pulled out and they drove to the local diner, as it was the only place in their small town that stayed open all night. They sat down at a table in the back and each ordered coffee and a slice of pie.

"I'm curious why you wanted to talk," Hannah said.

"I had fun tonight and wanted to get to know you a little more."

"What do you wanna know?"

"Why the pet store?"

"I've always loved dogs, really all animals. The pet stores we had were all boring. I decided I wanted something more fun and modern, and 'Rock the Fur' was born."

"Why the name?"

"I've been a metalhead all my life. I know I don't look like the typical rock fan, but it truly is my favorite music. I have a whole line of rock-themed pet products and I only play that type of music in my store."

"I'd love to come see it."

"I can't stop you."

"Can I ask you something more personal?"

"It's a free country."

"How come you were by yourself tonight?"

Hannah sighed. "I had a steady stream of boyfriends in high school. Not sure what changed after that but other than the occasional date, nothing. Guess I'm too plain for men to be interested."

"You're far from plain."

"Sure."

"You don't believe me?"

"No. I can only imagine the women you're used to, and I don't come close."

"No, you don't. You're much sexier."

Hannah snorted, knowing he was just trying to be nice. She'd seen pictures of his girlfriend and Hannah didn't hold a candle to her.

"My turn for a question," Hannah said after a few minutes of silence.

"Shoot."

"Why are you with me when you have that beautiful girlfriend?"

"She's a bitch."

"Then why stay with her?"

"Her father's the president of the record company I'm contracted with."

"Ah."

"She threatens to run to daddy every time she's unhappy."

"I'm sorry," Hannah said with a warm smile.

Mikael felt his heart start racing again. This woman was affecting him more than even he was prepared for. He could see Liza in his head again, but this time, he was able to ignore it. He was dreading the fact that she would be arriving in a couple days. Once she did, he would have to put Hannah out of his head.

"We're planning to have Dean and Alex give us a tour of the area tomorrow then everyone's going off on their own. Could I come see the store and maybe take you to dinner?"

"A date? But your girlfriend."

"It would be just as friends. I mean, if you'd like to be friends, that is."

"I would, so yes, I'll give you a tour of the shop and have dinner with you."

They finished their pie and got up to pay the check, then walked out to Hannah's car. She drove him back to his hotel. Before he got out, they exchanged cell numbers. Mikael told her he'd call her once he was back at his hotel and firm up their plans. Before she realized what was happening, he pulled head to his and kissed her passionately. He stopped as suddenly as he started, and apologized, then quickly got out of the car and walked toward the hotel. She waited until he was in his room before she pulled out and headed home, her mind and her heart racing a mile a minute.

Chapter Two

"Woof Woof."

"I can't believe it's only two," Hannah sighed to nobody. Mid-afternoon was usually the slowest time of the day at her shop. Hannah audibly exhaled, mostly from boredom, but also with some loneliness mixed in. She was in the longest dry spell of her life, relationship-wise. She could barely remember the last time she'd had sex with something that didn't require batteries. She used her lunch break to go down to the local adult shop and grab a new toy, which was sitting in a bag back in her office.

Getting to dance and talk with Mikael last night left her wanting more. When she got home from the diner, she laid in bed fantasizing about him, and boy were those fantasies steamy. Mikael was 6 feet of sexy, especially his long brown hair and beautiful sapphire eyes. He seemed a bit more on the modest side, but he had his shirt open just enough that Hannah could see a patch of chest hair peeking out, begging for her fingers. She would love to get a chance to see what else he was hiding under his clothes. She sighed audibly for the second time, though this was more out of loneliness, wishing she could see Mikael again. She was snapped out of her daydream by the sound of the bells over her door.

"Hey there, Sugartits," Mikael quipped.

"Well, if it isn't the one and only Sergeant Pepperballs!"

"Beatles fan?"

"Duh, who isn't?"

"You're a sassy little thing, aren't you?"

Winking, Hannah said, "I thought you were going to call me."

"I stopped by instead."

He wanted to kick himself the second that left his lips. *Of course you did, stupid. She can see you standing right in front of her,* he chastised himself. She was nice enough not to call him out on that.

"The shop's dead today, so how about that tour you wanted?"

A naughty smile appearing, he replied, "Let's do it."

Hannah went weak in the knees but quickly composed herself and walked Mikael around the store, showing him all the different displays, especially the rock section, which he loved. She was walking past her office when Cocoa gave a little bark, so Mikael peeked in. Cocoa immediately rolled onto her back which earned her some belly rubs. Hannah found herself wishing Mikael's hands were on her instead. If only life had those fairytale endings where Mikael would fall in love with her and she would finally get her happily ever after. They finished the tour and no additional customers had come in. They were standing up front near the register. All of a sudden, Hannah heard Mikael laughing hysterically.

"Are you okay?" she asked.

He was laughing so hard, he couldn't speak, so he pointed. She looked over and saw Cocoa standing there with something in her mouth. It took her a minute to realize what it was and when she did, she wished the floor would open up and suck her in. Cocoa was standing there with Hannah's brand new vibrator between her teeth. Hannah turned bright red, hoping with all her might the floor would open and swallow her in.

"Um, I can explain," she stammered.

"No need. They say self-care is important," he teased.

"Ha ha ha," she replied.

"New topic. You hungry?"

"Starving."

"You know the town, where should we go?"

"Depends what you're hungry for," she said.

He couldn't tell her what he really wanted, so he said, "I'm not picky. How about you?"

"Pizza's always good."

"I thought you wanted eggplant," he teased.

Hannah let out a little giggle and Mikael's heart skipped a beat.

"Seems dead today, so I'm gonna close early."

"Can I help?"

"Thanks, but I'm fine, do this every day,"

Mikael followed her as she took care of closing everything down, and his closeness was driving her crazy. She desperately wanted to grab him and kiss him but she knew she couldn't. She was almost grateful that his girlfriend would be coming. It would make it easier for her to stay away from him. If it wasn't one of the dearest friends getting married, she'd think about skipping the rest of the events. If only she could have found a date, she wouldn't feel so stupid being there. Once she had everything done, Hannah turned out all the lights.

They went to her favorite pizza place for dinner, hoping that none of their friends would see them, even though they were only friends. She didn't want anything getting back to Liza and cause drama at the wedding. She kept the conversation more on the casual side, focusing on Mikael's music career, and staying away from any personal stuff. Talking about life in the music business and some of the crazy stuff he saw had him laughing and seemed more like what she would have expected. By the end of the meal, she was laughing along with him, feeling more relaxed than when they arrived. Of course, she also had to endure some more teasing about the incident earlier, but luckily, she had as sick a sense of humor as he did.

They also discovered they had a lot of common interests, like hockey, comedy, and singing Karaoke. She figured Mikael would be way better than her, given he was a professional musician, but she still found it fun. She would love to do some of that stuff with him, but she knew that wouldn't be an option if he did live here, given he had a girlfriend, but hey, nothing wrong with dreaming.

Once they were done, Mikael grabbed the check. Hannah tried to pay half but he would hear none of that. They headed out to the parking lot and walked over to Hannah's car. Since Mikael had driven the rental van, she didn't have to drop him at the hotel so when they were done eating, she headed home. She got Cocoa's dinner ready then made herself a sandwich. After they both ate, she grabbed Cocoa's leash and so she could take her for a walk. Hannah lived in a quiet neighborhood of middle-class homes. Her house was a one-floor ranch style home with a heated garage attached. She had a sitting room, kitchen and small dining room, a living room, two bedrooms, and a nice big bathroom complete with a shower and a hot tub. If only she had a man to share it with, especially one particular man.

She knew this house would never be fancy enough for someone like Mikael. She could barely imagine the type of luxury he was used to, though she had at least somewhat of an idea when she saw Liza. Liza was model-thin, with short, stylish blonde hair and pretty blue eyes. Hannah looked in the mirror at her curvy figure, long, boring brown hair, and plain face, knowing Mikael would never be interested in her. Sure, he danced with her quite a bit when he was in town for the wedding, but she figured it was because he was alone and because he felt sorry for her.

She pulled up her playlist of Mikael's music on her phone as she walked, getting excited every time she heard his bass. She had watched countless videos of him playing, wishing it was her body that his fingers were playing. That was usually the point where she had to visit her "dirty" drawer and take care of her own business. It was those times when she was thankful that dogs can't talk. After her walk, she treated herself to a bowl of sympathy ice cream then sat down to read one of the many romance novels on her to be read list. If only she could experience what the heroines in her books did. She started fantasizing about acting out the naughty scenes in the book with Mikael. She especially loved books where the couples engaged in role-play. She always thought she would like to try that, but never felt comfortable enough with anyone to suggest it.

Once she was done, she headed off to bed, but of course she couldn't sleep. All she could do is lay there and look at the empty space next to her. If only that space could be filled with Mikael's naked body. There went those naughty thoughts again. She had to stop thinking like that. They were just friends. At this rate, she was going to need a ten-hour long cold shower. She finally was able to fall asleep, only to have her dreams filled with more naked images of Mikael.

The following morning, Hannah ran down to the store to put a sign on the door that she would be closed until Sunday due to the wedding. She was looking forward to the rehearsal dinner tonight, especially the chance to see Mikael. At least this time, it would be easier to keep her distance as his girlfriend would be there, so Mikael would be dancing with her instead. She was just getting ready to lock up and head back home when she saw Mikael.

"Hi," he said with a smile that almost made her pass out.

"Hey."

"I was hoping we could talk some more."

"Sure."

"Any suggestion where?"

"The park?"

"Okay."

They walked over to the park, as it was only about ten minutes away from her shop. There weren't a lot of people there, so they had their pick of benches. Mikael made sure he was right next to her, and their legs were touching, sending waves of electric heat throughout her body. She would have given anything for a repeat of that kiss. His voice snapped her back to reality.

"How come you don't have a man?"

"Yikes."

"Too personal?"

"More like pathetic."

"Tell me."

"Look at me. I'm not the type of woman men want."

"But you're sexy."

"Wheat bread is sexier than me."

"Not true."

"Right. I'm sure I don't hold a candle to those LA women."

"No, you're better."

"Sure."

They spent the next hour or so sharing stories about their youth and what led them down their current paths. Suddenly, Mikael look at his watch.

"Oh, shit."

"What?"

"Forgot to pick up Liza."

"Oh no."

He was about to answer when he saw Andy running over. Liza had been calling everyone looking for Mikael. They were all nice enough to cover for him. They told her the group was out sightseeing and lost track of time. She said she would get a cab and asked for directions to Alex's house. Since she was coming from Philly, they had time to get to Alex's before she did.

"Sorry, Hannah, I gotta go."

She waved as he and Andy raced back to the van. She sat a little while longer, hearing him say she was sexy over and over until she thought she was going to lose her mind. She decided to head home, grab a small snack then get herself ready for the dinner. She was nervous, both to see Mikael, and to see how much better looking Liza was than her. She knew for sure if not for Mikael only being here a short time, he would never have said she was sexy. He was safe, however, since he would be returning to California in a few days.

She gave Cocoa her dinner then took her for a quick walk, then got in the shower to get ready. She was an even bigger jumble of nerves than she was before. She just had to put that all aside and focus on her sweet friend Alex. She was so happy for her, even if she was a bit envious. Not to the point of wishing anything bad, but rather wishing she could find what Alex and Dean had. She knew it would never be with Mikael, and just wished it would be anyone at this point.

She opted for a simple yellow dress with short sleeves. She figured yellow would be plain enough that Mikael wouldn't give her a second look, especially with his hot LA girlfriend there. She pulled her hair back in a loose braid and grabbed a light jacket in case she needed it after the sun went down. Looking in the mirror, she knew that was the best she could hope to look, so she said goodbye to Cocoa and headed over to Alex's.

When Hannah arrived, she saw that Mikael was already there.

Sitting with him was a model-thin, leggy blonde with the most bored look Hannah had ever seen on her face. Seeing Liza, she knew there was no way Mikael truly thought she was sexy or that he would ever be interested in her. She walked past him to get to an empty seat by herself, but never noticed his eyes on her the whole time.

When it came time for dinner, everyone except Liza headed to the buffet line. Hannah could hear her demanding to be served. Being the sweet person she was, Alex went over to ask her what she wanted. Hannah didn't want to see her miss out on enjoying this night with Dean, so she headed over and sent Alex back to sit with Dean. She asked them what he wanted then headed to up to make them plates. Mikael got up and followed her.

"Sorry about her," he whispered.

"It's okay, happy to help."

She finished making Liza a plate then headed back to the table and handed it to her with a warm smile. She got nothing in return, not even a thank you, so she just quietly walked back to where she was sitting and ate by herself, while everyone else was with that special someone. She found herself fighting hard to suppress the tears that were threatening to spill over. She wished like hell just one man would find her worthy of love. She couldn't help but watch Dean and Alex together. It was heartwarming seeing how much they love each other.

After dinner was over came the time that Hannah was dreading most. Alex was directing all the couples to the dance floor, so that left Hannah as the spectator, as always. She noticed Mikael ask Liza to dance, but she refused, instead just sitting there with that sour look on her face. She was looking down in her lap, trying to avoid watching all the other couples enjoying themselves, and didn't see Mikael approaching. She jumped when she heard him speak.

"Would you like to dance?"

"But, Liza."

"She won't lower herself to dance."

"I'm sorry."

"Don't be, please just dance with me."

"Um, okay, I guess."

Hannah stood and walked behind Mikael to the dance floor. Her knees buckled when he took her into his arms, and she had to hold him to keep from going down. She saw a hint of a smile on his face, so she knew he noticed her reaction to him. What was it about this man? Why is he affecting me like this? Her mind and her heart were racing like they did whenever she was near him. At least with her plain yellow dress and even plainer looks, she knew he would only view her as a friend.

"You look hot tonight," he whispered in her ear.

His voice and his words sent shivers through her entire body, to the point that she shivered noticeably, then felt completely mortified, praying that he didn't notice. Just her luck, he did.

"Chilly?"

"Yeah."

He held her tighter, rubbing her arms with his strong hands. She definitely wasn't chilly anymore. Now she was afraid she would break out into a sweat at how hot he was getting her. Being with him was like being on a roller-coaster. She knew she should probably run as far as she could and never look back, but damn, she was enjoying being in his arms. They danced together the rest of the night, until Dean politely kicked everyone out. She said a quick goodnight to Mikael then went over and hugged Alex and Dean.

She was just pulling into her driveway when she saw headlights behind her. She got scared for a minute that someone had followed her until she recognized the rental van. Her stomach filled with butterflies when she saw Mikael get out and walk over to her.

"What're you doing here?"

"I needed to see you."

"Where does Liza think you are?"

"She's in a separate room. Don't ask."

"Oh."

"Can I come in?"

"Not sure that's the best idea."

"Fine, porch then?"

"Okay."

"Thanks again for tonight."

"No worries, Liza's used to a certain kind of treatment, I'm sure."

"No, thank you for the dance. It felt nice having someone in my arms."

"Like you don't have that every night," she said flippantly.

She saw Mikael wince and immediately regretted her words.

"Sorry, that was rude," she said quietly.

"Liza hasn't touched me since we met."

"Then why is she with you?"

"Money."

"Oh, I'm so sorry. You deserve better."

"I deserve you."

"Don't be silly."

"You look so beautiful tonight. Yellow suits you."

Hannah was thankful it was dark, so he couldn't see her blushing.

"Thanks."

"I better head back before anyone notices."

"Yeah, plus I'm exhausted."

"See you at the wedding."

"Goodnight, Mikael."

"Night."

Chapter Three

Hannah was awakened by the sun's rays gleaming in through her windows, showing all the dust she hadn't had time to clean up. She fed Cocoa, ate a quick bowl of cereal, then took Cocoa for a long walk in hopes of clearing her head. A couple hours later, she headed back home, and sat down on the couch. She put her head back for a minute and next thing she knew, she was waking up two hours later. She now had to rush and grab a shower then get ready to head to the wedding.

She decided on another yellow dress, since Mikael liked the first one so much. She had to admit, she kinda liked what she saw in the mirror. When Hannah arrived, she took a seat by herself. When Dean and his groomsmen walked in and Hannah's jaw dropped. Mikael looked so handsome. The look on Dean's face when he saw Alex was beautiful. Hannah wished someone would look at her like that someday.

Mikael found himself unable to take his eyes off the vision in yellow. He started picturing his wedding, and he definitely didn't see Liza. He wished more than anything in this world he could get out of his relationship with her. So lost in his thoughts, he missed most of the ceremony. The bridal party went off to take pictures, but all Mikael wanted was to get back to his beautiful flower.

The group rejoined the party as the hors d'oeuvres were winding down. Mikael managed to grab a couple before the servers stopped to get ready for dinner. He took his spot at the bridal table, grateful to have a clear line of site to Hannah. He felt completely comfortable around Hannah and he wanted to spend as much time with her as he could before he returned to California and out of her life. Her friendship was definitely making it hard to leave, but he knew he had to get back to LA.

Once dinner was done, the DJ announced that it was time for dancing. Liza, of course, refused, which actually Mikael was glad about. This would be his last chance to dance with Hannah. He walked over to her table, and asked her to dance, and this time, she agreed without hesitation.

"You look even more stunning than last night," Mikael said.

"I look like Big Bird."

"Stop that. You're perfect."

"Sure I am."

"I hate hearing you talk like that."

"Fine, I'll go sit and leave you alone."

"That's not what I meant. Please stay with me."

"Why? I really don't get what you like about me."

"You're kindness for one," he lamented.

She smiled. "You're sweet."

"I also really like dancing with you," he cooed.

"Mmm, I like you, I mean dancing with you," she whispered.

"I can't believe I have to leave tomorrow."

"I really wish you didn't."

"I'll miss you."

"I have to admit, I'll miss you too."

"Can we stay friends even after I'm back in LA?"

"Are you sure that won't be a problem?"

"The she-devil won't care. I could really use a friend."

"Me too, I don't have many of those, especially men."

"A beauty like you?"

"Funny."

"You're beautiful whether you believe it or not."

"I guess," she said, her cheeks reddening.

Mikael pulled her in closer, his arms tightly circled around her waist.

Wrapping her arms around his strong chest, she laid her head on his shoulder, completely lost in the moment. She was thankful that several slow songs in a row played before the DJ sped things up.

"I wish I could stay in your arms forever," she murmured.

"I do too. Holding you feels so right. But I know it's wrong as long as I'm with her."

They danced together for the rest of the night while Liza sat by herself, looking like she was smelling a fart. The night flew by way too fast, and Hannah felt an intense sadness that this would be the last time she would see Mikael. She walked over to say goodbye to the newlyweds. She loved seeing her friend so happy, and hoped maybe someday it would be her turn. As they hugged, Alex whispered in Hannah's ear.

"I saw you with Mikael. I think he likes you."

Hannah didn't respond, she just congratulated her then moved on to hug Dean, who also whispered to her.

"You and Mikael fit."

Again, she didn't respond, instead walking to her car and starting towards home. Feeling restless, she took a turn and headed to the park to take a walk and try to clear her head. As she was walking, she heard her phone indicate a text had come in. She should have known it would be Mikael.

"Thank you for the dance. Miss you already."

She texted back a simple, *"You're welcome."*

She put her phone away and continued her walk. She felt sad that she wasn't going to see Mikael in person after tonight. He would board a plane in the morning and fly out of her life for good. She sat down on a bench and burst into tears. She had no idea why she was reacting like this, and nobody she could even talk to about it. Alex was her only friend and she would be leaving for her honeymoon in the morning. She certainly couldn't talk to Mikael, since he was the cause of her anguish. That left her one person, and honestly, her preference since she knew her secret would stay safe.

She got back in her car and drove home. Cocoa jumped up when she heard the door open and ran over to Hannah, as if it had been years since they'd last seen each other. Hannah sat down on her couch, and

Cocoa jumped up and laid next to her, laying her head in Hannah's lap. Looking at her beloved dog, she confided in her.

"What am I going to do? I wanted him to stay more than anything."

Cocoa moved closer to her, as if she understood Hannah's pain. Having her there made Hannah feel a little better, but didn't remove that empty feeling in her heart. She missed Mikael more than she thought she would and just hoped the pain would become more bearable as time went on. Hannah ended up falling asleep on her couch for a little while. When she woke up she put Cocoa out for one last bathroom break then headed off to bed.

She allowed herself to sleep in since she decided to wait until Monday to re-open the store. She wasn't sure what her mental state would be after the wedding and with Mikael leaving, so she figured a quiet day at home would be just what she needed. Starting fresh on Monday would help her be more focused on work and less on him. She turned on her phone and had several missed texts from Mikael, all begging her to come see him one last time. She knew by now he would be in the air so she didn't bother texting back. No point, she thought, as I'm sure he'll forget all about me when he gets home, even if she would never forget him.

While Hannah was spending another day alone, Mikael wished he was too. Instead, he was stuck sitting there listening to Liza go on and on about the multitude of things she hated about the airport, the flight, the attendants, and every other thing she could possibly bitch about. He wanted noting more than to tell her to shut the fuck up, but he stayed silent. He leaned back, shut his eyes, and let images of Hannah filled his head. He couldn't forget seeing her in that yellow dress at the wedding, her sexy breasts showing just enough to drive him wild. He tried with no luck to see her one last time before he left, but she wouldn't agree.

"Mikael!"

Liza's shrill voice pierced the air and interrupted his daydream about the oh-so-sexy Hannah. If he'd had a pencil, he would have popped both his eardrums so he'd never have to hear that damn screech again.

"I've been talking to you? Where the hell were you?"

"Nowhere. Just tired."

"Whatever. I'm thirsty."

"Call the attendant."

"Maybe I should call daddy instead."

"Fine. Fuck."

Mikael pressed the button to call the attendant and ordered a mineral water for the banshee. When she brought the water, the attendant gave Mikael a sympathetic look.

"Can I bring you anything, sir?"

He smiled and responded, "No, thank you."

Lately, it seemed that if he wasn't spending his time waiting on her, he was spending it apologizing or trying to make up for her nasty attitude. Now that she had her water, Liza put her head back to rest, allowing Mikael to go back to thinking about Hannah. He found himself picturing what it would be like to strip her down and make love to her. He had to be careful that his fantasies didn't activate his launch sequence. He didn't want to have to explain away a hard-on, especially with the loudmouth sitting next to him. He heard a text come into his phone and he got excited, thinking it was Hannah. The text turned out to be from Andy.

"Thinking about Hannah?"

"No"

"Your nose is growing, and maybe your dick too."

"Sure"

"Your face says otherwise"

"Fuck off"

He heard Andy and Lizzie laughing as they read his responses. He actually let himself laugh a little too. Hannah was bringing out his old self and it felt good. Of course, it was short-lived with the she-devil sitting next to him. She stirred when she heard him laughing.

"Really, asshole. You just woke me up."

"Sorry."

"Whatever. Just shut up."

She closed her eyes again, as Mikael sat there with a sullen look on his face. Lizzie and Andy turned around and mouthed a sorry with sympathetic looks on their faces. Great, all I am is someone for everyone to pity. I'm fucking sick of feeling this way, he thought to himself. Something definitely changed in him during his trip to Pennsylvania, largely due to meeting Hannah, but also seeing how much happier Dean was. Maybe I should move there too. He didn't give it any more thought then as the captain announced for everyone to buckle up as they prepared for final descent. Getting ready to land in LA made him feel more miserable than ever.

Once they landed and grabbed their luggage, Damon and Andy grabbed a ride for them and their wives. Mikael decided to get a separate one for him and Liza so nobody else had to put up with her. They quietly thanked him and wished him luck. If only they knew the plans that were starting to formulate in his head. When they got home, Liza announced she was going to the spa to get "the stink of farm" off her. Mikael was just as glad to get rid of her for a while since he had work to do.

After hell on heels stomped out the door and got in her car, he fired up his laptop and searched for a Pennsylvania real estate company. He was hoping he would find something not too far from Hannah. The way she behaved at the rehearsal dinner and wedding was the nail in the coffin as far as their relationship went. He knew his friends would never understand his decision, but they also didn't know the extent of the hell Liza put him through.

Not only her demanding attitude and her ability to spend money at record speed, but they hadn't been intimate in over a year. She wasn't kind about it either, saying things like she didn't want his stink on her or that he was beneath touching her, as if her pussy was made of twenty-four karat gold or something. Still, Mikael remained faithful, his only slip being kissing Hannah. He had to admit he found himself excited to tell Liza he was leaving, but he knew he needed to wait until he had everything secured.

He took a quick peek at his secret bank account, happy that he had plenty of money aside to be able to pay cash for the home. He was also thankful Liza didn't know about that account or it would be empty. He didn't even care at this point that he would likely have to pay something to get out of his contract, as he valued his sanity more. That coupled with the fact that he had fallen for Hannah made it all worth it.

After a couple hours of searching, he found a house that he loved and put in a bid. He knew it would be a while before he heard anything so he shut his laptop down and locked up his office. He took Leo outside and sat on the back porch, enjoying the warm sun. His mind immediately wandered to Hannah and he wondered what she was doing and if she was thinking of him. He grabbed his phone to check his social media. He had sent a friend request to Hannah, and smiled when he saw she'd accepted it.

He found himself scrolling through her page, trying to get to know more about her life. A lot of her posts were pictures of Cocoa, as well as a lot of rock music videos. He also saw several pictures from the wedding, including one of the two of them dancing. He saved that one to his phone, so he could look at her whenever he wanted. Not that she wasn't always in his head, but he couldn't get enough of seeing her in that sexy yellow dress.

Dinnertime arrived and Liza still wasn't home, so he grabbed himself something to eat then sat down to watch a movie. He honestly didn't care if she stayed out all night. He wouldn't be her problem for much longer. He knew she would never want to move away from LA, so he was counting on her dumping him once he was ready to move. A little while later, his phone rang. A representative from the real estate company was on the other end with some damn good news. His bid was accepted, so the house was his. He let them know he was currently living in LA, but that he would fly out for settlement once that was scheduled. The agent let him know she'd be back in touch with him soon.

His first thought was to call Hannah and tell her, but he decided instead that he would surprise her once he was there to stay. He really needed to tell someone, so he called Andy. He came clean about everything that Liza had been putting him through and it felt good getting it off his chest.

"Dude, I knew it was bad, but I had no idea it was that bad."

"So you get why I'm leaving?"

"Same thing I told Dean, do what you feel is best for you, I watched you with Hannah and I could tell something was happening there."

"I wish she felt it too."

"She did. Lizzie is amazing at reading people and she could see clearly that Hannah has feelings for you."

"If only."

"Don't give up, you deserve someone like her."

"Thanks man. One favor, keep this under your hat, except for Lizzie, please."

"You got it. Anything you need, yell."

"Thanks. Later, man."

"Later."

After he disconnected with Andy, he went back on Hannah's profile and clicked the button to send her a direct message.

"Hey. Hope all is good. Miss you."

When he didn't get a response right away, he put his phone in his pocket and watched the rest of the movie he had on. When it was over, he put his favorite late night talk show on then headed to bed. Liza still hadn't come home. Mikael figured she was off having an affair but he truly didn't give a fuck. Let someone else put up with her shit. He just had to bide his time until his settlement got scheduled. He did one last thing before he fell asleep and hoped she would love it.

Chapter Four

Shortly after Hannah arrived at work, the local florist stopped by with a delivery. Tears filled Hannah's eyes when she read the card.

"Two dozen yellow roses for my stunning dance partner. Never have I seen yellow look quite as beautiful as you in that dress. I miss you."

She unwrapped the vase and put it on the counter. As much as the flowers made her smile, they also left her with a dull ache in her belly. She missed Mikael way more than she thought she would. She was completely lost in her thoughts and never heard her employee Kurt come in.

"Good Morning, Hannah," he boomed.

Hannah gasped then replied, "Good Morning."

"Where were you just now and does it have anything to do with those?"

"Just thinking, and no, they're from a friend."

"A friend sends you two dozen roses?"

"What's that supposed to mean?" she snapped.

"Whoa, just teasing."

"I'm sorry. Not quite myself this morning."

"No worries. I'm here if you need an ear."

"Thanks."

Meanwhile, on the other side of the country, Mikael got a call from the his real estate agent letting him know settlement would be in a month. The current owners were being relocated as one of them received a promotion at work, so they needed to move fairly quickly. Mikael noted the date and time, thanked the agent then disconnected. He immediately booked himself a flight and hotel for the day before the meeting. Liza was spending very little time at the house these days, giving him ample time to start packing. He rented a storage unit so that when he was ready, the moving company could just go there and load everything. On the rare occasions Liza was home, she didn't even notice how much of his stuff was no longer there. Now all that was left was deciding when to tell her. He looked at his phone, but still hadn't seen a response from Hannah and wondered what she was doing.

Hannah was sitting behind the counter at the pet store reviewing her inventory when she heard her phone ping. She looked down and saw that Mikael had responded that he missed her. She missed him too, way more than she wanted to admit, especially because it brought back that hollow ache in the pit of her stomach again. She decided not to respond right now and wait to see if she got another message. At least being here at work, she could focus on something other than missing him. Her phone pinged again.

"Can we have a video call later?"

"I guess."

"Text me when you're ready."

"Okay."

As soon as she put her phone down, she started having second thoughts but she didn't want to hurt his feelings. She had to admit she was actually looking forward to seeing him again, but at least this time, she wouldn't have to worry about him touching or kissing her. She wanted him to without question, but She couldn't. The rest of her day went fast, as there was a steady stream of customers. Once she closed up, she started to head home. She decided to make a detour to the dog park so Cocoa could run a little bit before they retired for the night.

Nobody was there that night, so she played with Cocoa for about an hour then stopped to grab a quick dinner. She wanted to shower and look as presentable as possible for her call with Mikael. She wasn't sure why it was so important to her how she looked when they were just friends. After her shower, she put on jeans and a low-cut yellow t-shirt, since she knew Mikael liked the yellow dress so much. When she was ready, she texted Mikael. He must have been waiting by the phone, as a minute later, she got a video call. She answered and saw Mikael's handsome face.

"Hey, beautiful," Mikael said with a big smile.

Blushing, she replied, "Hello. Thank you so much for the beautiful flowers."

"My pleasure. How are ya?"

"The store has been busy."

"Great, but I asked how you were."

"Fine."

"Give me a little more than that."

"I miss you."

Mikael saw a sadness sweep across her beautiful face.

"I miss you too."

She moved back from the phone a little and Mikael saw her shirt. His jaw dropped when he saw her breasts peeking out over the top of a low cut yellow shirt. Damn, she was gorgeous. He was definitely a breast guy and he sure couldn't take his eyes off hers. He really wanted to see her completely naked, wanted to taste her skin, wanted to have his dick inside her as she called his name. He suddenly remembered he was on a video chat with her and hoped that he didn't give any of his thoughts away. If he did, she was nice enough not to mention it.

"What have you been up to, other than the store?"

She certainly couldn't tell him how much time she'd spent thinking of him, and especially what she usually ended up doing when the naughty thoughts got her too worked up.

"Either spending time with Cocoa, reading or watching TV. Nothing all that exciting. What about you?"

"Mostly just hiding from Liza," he said only half-jokingly.

"I'm sorry. Still giving you a hard time?"

"Non-stop. Some days, I just want to walk away, but I'm stuck."

"I wish there was a way you could get away from her without losing your contract."

"Me too."

"Not trying to be nosy, but have you talked to her dad?"

"I thought about it, but it didn't seem right."

"I guess. How much longer is the contract?"

"Five years."

"Oh fuck, that's a long time."

Mikael had never heard her talk like that before, and he definitely liked it. He was always turned on by dirty talk, in or out of the bedroom, and he felt something stirring in his jeans. He was grateful she could only see him from the neck up. He took a couple of deep breaths, trying to calm the beast, but he had a feeling he would have to take care of business after their call.

"Never heard you use that word before."

"Sorry."

"Don't be, it's sexy."

"Oh," she said as her cheeks reddened.

He desperately wanted to tell her his news, but he had already made up his mind that he was going to surprise her when he arrived, so he kept it to himself. He was about to say something else when he heard the front door slam.

"Shit, Liza's home."

"Don't let her catch you. We can talk another time."

Before he had a chance to respond, he had to disconnect as he heard the clicking of her heels getting closer to his office. He quick turned on his laptop and opened some of this music files to make it look like he'd been working. He needed to make sure Liza didn't figure out he was leaving California in a month. She slammed the office door open.

"Dinner."

"Food's in the kitchen."

"I know where it is."

"Then go get some."

He wanted to tell her to fuck off, but he couldn't risk blowing his news until he was ready to tell her.

"Fine."

He walked to the kitchen and grabbed a box of cereal and a bowl, and put it front of her.

"Enjoy."

Before she could say anything, he turned and walked out of the kitchen, heading straight for the shower. He knew she would never follow him there, so he would get some peace and quiet. He turned the water as hot as he could stand it then stared lathering up. The worse Liza treated him, the more he was glad he was moving. He also decided that even if they split and Hannah was still single, the best he could give her was friendship. He just didn't want to deal with another relationship. The next four weeks flew by, as he kept himself busy. Two days before the move, he decided it was time to tell Liza. He walked into the living room where she was sitting on the couch.

"Need to tell you something," he said, grinning from ear to ear.

"Make it quick."

"I'm moving."

"I beg your pardon."

"You heard me."

"But I like this house."

"Good for you."

"I don't wanna move."

"Who said you were? I said I was moving."

'Where?"

"Pennsylvania."

"What the hell for?"

"I'm sick of LA. I need a change."

"Fine. When do we leave?"

"Again, who said we?"

"I'm going or I call daddy."

"Fuck. You hated it there."

"I'll learn to deal."

"Get the fuck packing then. I fly out in two days. If you're not ready, you can stay the fuck here."

She stomped off to go pack, while he sat and buried his head in his hands. He never fucking thought she'd want to go with him. He took the rest of his boxes to storage as the moving company would be picking them up in the morning. He returned home and packed a suitcase to hold him over until his stuff arrived. He didn't tell her about the movers. She could figure out what do with her stuff on her own. She also couldn't get a flight until after his settlement meeting, so at least he could do that in peace. He spent the next couple of days getting everything ready for his departure, including selling his car, and finalizing arrangements with the moving company.

He was overjoyed when he woke up the morning of his flight. It would be nice to get a few days away from Liza, plus he couldn't wait to surprise Hannah. He had purchased first class tickets, and bought two seats so he could put Leo in his carrier on the seat next to him. Before he knew it, he was touching down in Philly. He couldn't help but notice the difference in the weather. He didn't mind, as it was a refreshing change from LA. After he grabbed his luggage, he picked up his rental car and drove to Lancaster.

Meanwhile, Mikael was sitting in his hotel room, going over his plan for the next day. He had his settlement meeting the next morning then he planned to visit the pet shop and tell Hannah the news. He hadn't been able to stop thinking about her since the first time he met her. She couldn't have any more opposite Liza, and that was honestly his favorite thing about her. She was softer and kinder, and treated people the way they should be treated. He had also discovered through social media that they had a lot more in common than he realized. It would be nice to have a friend to do things with.

The next morning, he ordered room service for breakfast, then got ready to head to his meeting. Everything went smoothly and he left there owning a home in the beautiful state of Pennsylvania. The only thing he could think about now was racing over to the shop to tell Hannah. When he went in, he didn't see her right away so he started walking each aisle until he spotted her. She had her back to him, so he approached her.

"Excuse me, miss, could I get some assistance?"

Hannah turned around and her eyes went wide.

"What are you doing here?"

Mikael held up a piece of paper.

"I just made settlement on a house."

"Here?"

"Yep."

"I don't understand."

"Like Dean, I needed a change of scenery. Seeing how much he loved it out here, I knew it was the right place for me too."

'Are you alone?"

"Right now. Liza will be here tomorrow."

Hannah's face fell.

"Congratulations. Happy for you."

"You wanna celebrate with dinner tonight?"

"No."

"Why not?"

"Liza's still you girlfriend, right?"

"Yep, but-"

"Then no. I need to get back to work."

"We're friends. Why can't we go out?"

Not feeling up to arguing, she said, "Fine. We can go."

"I'll be back at closing time to pick you up."

"I'll need to take Cocoa home first, so I'll meet you at the diner."

"Okay, see you then."

The rest of the day was fairly busy. When she got home, Mikael was sitting in her driveway waiting for her.

"I thought we were meeting at the diner," she said.

"Wanted to make sure you wouldn't bail on me. Since I'm here, I'll drive."

"Fine."

She took Cocoa inside, got her dinner ready then walked over to his car. They drove over to the diner and sat at a table in the back. After they ordered, an awkward silence settled over their table, until Hannah finally spoke.

"I can't believe you're here."

"Me either. It hasn't yet sunk in. Liza is pissed."

"Isn't she always? I'm sorry, that was rude?"

"Not rude and completely true. I never thought she'd come."

"What if she calls her dad?"

"Then I lose my contract. At this point, I don't give a fuck."

"But the money you'd lose."

"It's not worth my sanity."

33

"I guess you're right. Maybe she'll hate and just leave."

"Honestly, that's what I'm hoping."

The waiter brought their coffee and food. Hannah reached for a sugar packet.

"Want me to do that, Sugartits?" he teased.

"So fuckin' funny," she replied, sticking her tongue out.

One look at the tongue and he felt his dick stirring. Down boy, he commanded himself. They both reached for the pepper at the same time. Their hands brushed, sending a jolt of electricity through them both. She wanted him more than anything, but she knew that would never be a possibility. After the finished eating, Mikael paid their check then drove her home.

"Thanks for tonight," he said.

"You're welcome."

"Can we do it again sometime?"

"I don't think so, not with Liza here."

"I guess you're right."

"I really am happy for you. Take care," she sighed.

"You too," he whispered.

Feeling tears in his eyes, he quickly turned and got in his car without another word. He drove away but stopped a couple streets over and buried his head in his hands. He almost went back, but he knew he couldn't. Not with the she-devil coming tomorrow. He drove the rest of the way to his hotel and went right to bed. Of course, sleep eluded him, his mind consumed with missing Hannah.

He got up early the next morning and headed to Philly to pick up Liza at the airport. He certainly wasn't looking forward to seeing her or spending that two hour car ride back to Lancaster with her. Maybe she got laryngitis, he thought to himself. No such luck. She was her usual nasty self from the second she got in his rental car to the second he pulled up at the hotel. He stopped at the front of the main entrance to drop her off.

"I'll wait here until you check in then drive you to your room."

Without a word, she got out of the car and stormed into the lobby. About ten minutes later she came back out, eyes blazing with anger and got back in the car, slamming the door behind her.

"What happened?"

"They said they didn't have a room under my name."

"Did you get a confirmation when you booked it?"

"What do you mean when I booked it?"

"I told you to make your own travel arrangements."

"I thought you meant a plane ticket."

"Nope."

"Great, now I don't have a damn room, as they're full. Give me your key."

"For what?"

"I'm taking that room."

"You can stay in the room, but I'm not leaving."

"Whatever. Let's just go."

She rode the entire way to the room with her arms folded across her chest like an insolent child who didn't get her way, pretty much how she always acted. They went inside and Liza plopped down on the couch, pouting. He really was getting sick of her. If it wasn't for that fuckin' contract she held over his head, he would have put her on the first plane back to LA or hell, whichever.

"Hungry?"

"Nope," she said, still pouting.

"Okay, I'm heading out to grab some dinner."

"What about me?"

"You just said you weren't hungry."

"Whatever."

Mikael turned and walked out to his car then drove to the local diner. He was hoping he would possibly see Hannah there, but no such luck. He ate some dinner then drove by the pet shop but it was already closed so he headed back to the hotel. A week later, Mikael got a call from the real estate agent letting him know the former owners had finished moving, so the house was his. He checked out of the hotel and he and Liza headed to their new home. He wished it was Hannah he was bringing here instead. Liza, of course, hated it, but what the fuck else was new.

The moving company arrived the next morning. Mikael went outside to warn them about the she-devil and her attitude. They all commiserated with him, as they've all known women like her. She of course was rude to them so after about an hour, Mikael told them he was taking her to the park and to just lock the door when they were done. They thanked him profusely.

Mikael drove her to the park and they walked to an empty bench. She made it a whole 30 seconds before she lit into him.

"Why the fuck did you make me come back here," Liza angrily shouted.

"I saw how much leaving LA helped Dean and I wanted that too," Mikael responded.

'Well, this sucks."

"Just give it time, you'll learn to like it."

"I wanna go home."

"We can go once the movers have finished unloading everything."

"That's not home. I mean home to LA."

"Go then."

"What about you?"

"I'm staying here."

"Oh, so I see I'm gonna have to call daddy."

That was the last straw and Mikael snapped.

"Fucking call him then," he shouted. "No wait, fuck that. I'll fuckin' call him."

Before she could respond, Mikael dialed her father, who picked up after a couple rings. Mikael put the phone on speaker so Liza could hear everything.

"Hey, Mikael. How's the East Coast treating you?"

'I love it here, however I do have a problem."

"What's that?"

"I apologize in advance, but your spoiled brat of a daughter."

"She is, isn't she. Thank you for taking her all the way across the country and out of my hair. What'd she do?"

"She's demanding that we move back to LA, but I'm happy here, so I'm calling to tell you that I need to break my contract."

"Why would you need to do that?"

"Because I know if she's unhappy, you'll punish me by dissolving my contract."

"Who told you that?"

"Liza."

"First off, I never said that. Second, that would be illegal."

"So, let me get this straight, I no longer have to kiss her ass?"

"No you most certainly do not."

"You just made me the happiest man in the world. I need to take care of something."

Laughing, he said, "Goodbye and good luck."

Mikael disconnected, stood up and faced Liza, the biggest smile ever on his face.

"Bitch, it's over. Your stuff will be out front of my house. Have a miserable flight home and an even more miserable life."

Before she could respond, he turned and walked to his car, got in and drove home. He went to bed and had the best night's sleep of his life, finally free of the hell on heels.

Chapter Five

When he woke up in the morning, he was feeling a little down. Despite the way Liza had treated him, it still hurt when a relationship didn't work out. He found himself in need of a friend, so he got in his car and drove to Hannah's house. He knocked on her door when he arrived. She opened the door and Cocoa came bounding out to see him. He knelt down and petted her while Hannah stood there, a concerned look on her face.

"You seem a bit down this morning," she said.

"Liza and I split yesterday. I know I should be elated, but it's still hard when a relationship ends."

She sat down on one of the chairs on her porch and he walked over and sat next to him.

"I'm so sorry. Tell me what happened."

He told Hannah the story about what happened in the park and that he had never intended to bring her here in the first place. He was surprised she wanted to go and he thought she would have dumped him. He also told her that it was all lies that she could get her father to dissolve his contract.

"So now, I'm still with contract but without her."

"That's a good thing. What are you going to do now?"

"For right now, I just want to be single. After the hell she put me through, I need a break."

"I understand. I'm always here if you need a friend."

"That's what I was hoping. I like that we have so many common interests, so I thought we could hang out more often."

"I'd love to. Are you up for some fun tonight?"

"What'd you have in mind?"

"I have an extra ticket to the hockey game. Care to join me?"

"Yeah, let's do it. Wanna grab dinner on the way?"

'Yeah. Speaking of food, did you have breakfast yet?"

"No and I'm starving."

"You like French toast?"

"One of my favorites."

"Come on in. I have coffee ready."

Mikael sat at Hannah's kitchen table while she cooked. This was definitely a nice change. It had always been him doing everything for Liza, so it was nice to have someone take care of him. A short while later, Hannah laid two plates on the table and sat down across from him. The French toast smelled delicious and tasted even better. That combined with great company left him feeling good.

"This is really good. Thank you."

"My pleasure," she said, smiling.

He felt his heart skip a beat when she smiled at him, but quickly pushed that aside. He knew for sure a relationship was the last thing he wanted. Despite telling himself that, he was having a hard time taking his eyes off her. He tried to focus on something else.

"So, what time should we leave tonight?"

"I'm closing at 4 today and just need time to shower and change. Will 5 work for you?"

"Sounds like a plan."

She started clearing the table to clean the dishes before she left for work. He got up to help her. Despite her best effort, he wouldn't let her clean up after she cooked, so he washed and dried the dishes for her, so she could get Cocoa her breakfast then finish getting ready. He walked her to her car.

"Thanks again for breakfast."

"You're welcome. I'll pick you up at 5, just text me your address."

"I'll drive, so I'll pick you up here."

"That works. Can't wait."

"Me either."

Hannah opened the pet store and immediately had customers start filtering in. On days like this, she was grateful for her employees. Kurt helped her at the shop and Amanda ran her booth at the local farmer's market. She loved being busy, as it made the day go faster. She was also in an especially good mood, looking forward to the game tonight. She loved going to games but usually ended up going alone. She always had fun, as she would chat with whoever was sitting around her, but it would be different being there with a friend. She locked up a little after four and headed home. After a quick shower, she thew on a pair of jeans, white t-shirt and her favorite hockey jersey. Mikael arrived a little before five and they headed out.

"Anywhere special you want to eat?" she asked.

"No. Still learning the lay of the land, so I'll have to trust you for now."

She gave him directions to her favorites sports bar. They each ordered a burger, fries, and a beer. Mikael had always found it sexy when a woman was willing to down a beer and eat something other than a salad. He loved that Hannah finished every last bite and let a belch slip. She turned beet red and apologized. Mikael had found it endearing as opposed to disgusting. They arrived at the arena and headed to their seats. Hannah had been a season ticket holder for years, and had seats right along the glass at center ice.

Even though this was a minor league game, where he was used to attending NHL games, he still had an amazing time. Hannah knew her shit when it came to hockey. Nothing was worse than being with someone who had no clue and kept asking questions. They had a great time and to top it off, her team won. After the game, they stopped at the arena bar to celebrate with some of the other fans before they headed back to her house.

"Ever been to a pro game?" he asked.

"A few times, but it's a long drive when I have to work the next day. I've been a fan of the Philly team since I was a kid."

"I went to the LA games a lot, always in the VIP section."

"That would be my dream, especially if I got to meet any of the players."

Mikael made a mental note to see if he could call in a favor and make that happen for her. They drove back to her house and he walked her to her door. She sat down on the porch and he joined her.

"Mind if I hang out here for a bit?"

"Not at all, just let me go get Cocoa. I'm sure she needs to at least pee."

"Of course."

Cocoa came out and right over to him. Hannah followed her with a beer in each hand. She sat down and handed one to Mikael. Cocoa rolled onto her back at his feet. She definitely seemed to be taking a liking to him. After a few minutes of belly rubs, she trotted down the grass to do her business. He ended up staying for a couple of hours, as they talked and laughed like two old friends. He felt like his old self again and was grateful to her for helping coax that out of him. They both started yawning, so he got up to head to his car. Before he got in, he gave her a quick hug, and felt a weird sensation travel through his body. He blamed the beer and pushed it out of his head.

"Thanks for tonight. I needed to take my mind off Liza."

"I had fun too. Thanks for driving."

"You bet. Talk to you soon."

"Definitely. Good night."

"Night, Hannah."

She called Cocoa to come in then headed inside herself. Mikael waited until she shut and locked her door before he pulled out. He headed home and went right to bed, his dreams filled with some naughty images of his friend.

He spent the next several days finishing up the work he wanted to do in the house then started unpacking the rest of his boxes. He had mostly been unpacking only as he needed something, but really wanted to get the rest of the boxes out of the house. He was in the back of the house when he heard the doorbell ring. He walked out and was elated to see Dean and Alex standing there.

"I'm surprised to see you two dressed," he said laughing.

"Very funny," Dean replied. "It was one time you all caught us in robes."

Alex just gave him the finger and stuck her tongue out. Dean hugged her, and Mikael could see the love between them. That was something he never got with Liza and at this point didn't expect to ever get.

"Where's Liza?" Dean asked.

"I dumped that bitch."

"Holy shit, dude! What about the contract?"

"Turns out she was lying."

"What happened?" Alex asked.

Mikael told them the story about the day in the park and by the end of the story they were all laughing, especially about how her father reacted. It was safe to say nobody was sorry to see her out of Mikael's life. Alex excused herself to take a walk around the property, so the guys could chat.

"What you been up to since you got back?"

"Mostly just work around here. Last night, I went to the hockey game."

"You shoulda called, I would have gone so you weren't by yourself."

"I wasn't."

Dean raised an eyebrow and asked, "Hmmm, were you with a certain hot pet store owner?"

"I was with my *friend* Hannah."

Dean caught his emphasis on the word friend so he didn't push it, but he saw the way they were looking at each when they danced at the wedding. He swore there was something between them, but maybe he misread and they were really just friends.

"So, any plans tonight?"

"Nope."

"There's Karaoke at the club tonight. Care to join me & Alex?"

"Why not. Mind if I invite someone?"

"Of course I don't mind if Hannah comes."

"Knock it off asshole. We're friends."

"Yes, sir," Dean mocked.

Alex returned a few minutes later, so Mikael gave them a tour of the inside. The house had a living room, kitchen, dining room, and half-bathroom on the first floor. Upstairs was a full bathroom complete with a soaking tub, and three bedrooms. There was also a finished basement, which Mikael was planning on turning into a game and music room. He had a jukebox that he brought with him and would finish the room off with a pool table, which he had on order. He also put in a full bar. He couldn't wait until the pool table was in so he could throw a party.

After the tour, they firmed up their plans for the evening. Alex was happy to find out he would be asking Hannah to join them. She hoped that something was brewing there, as she knew how lonely her friend had been. They both hugged Mikael, congratulated him on the house and the move, then headed home. Once they were gone, he got in his car to head down to Hannah's store and ask her in person about tonight. He got there just as she was getting ready to break for lunch, leaving Kurt to handle things while she was gone. He waved when he saw her look his way.

"Hi Mikael. I was just heading out to grab some lunch."

"Want company?"

"Of course. Pizza okay?"

"Yeah."

They walked to the pizza place that was a couple stores down from hers and went inside. The lunch rush was over, so they had their choice of tables. They each ordered a couple slices and a soda then sat down and waited.

"Dean and Alex stopped by this morning to invite me to Karaoke at the club tonight. Care to join us?"

"I'd love to."

"Cool. I'm meeting them at the club at 7. I'll pick you up if you want and we could grab dinner on the way."

"I don't mind driving."

"I know, but this is helping me get to know where everything is."

"Got it. What time were you thinking?"

"Does 6 give you enough time after you close?"

"Yeah, that works."

"Can't wait," he said with a smile.

Returning the smile, she replied, "Me either."

After they finished lunch, they walked back to the store. Mikael came in and grabbed a couple things he needed for Leo then headed home. He was really excited for tonight, surprisingly so in fact. He wondered what that was all about. Probably just the newness of everything going on, he thought to himself, as images of Hannah floated through his head. He couldn't wait to see her up there singing tonight since she said she had so much fun doing it, even if, in her words, she was lousy.

He headed home to do some more work in the house. The only room he really needed to change some stuff in was the bathroom. He decided he wanted more of a beachy feel to it, so he headed to grab some teal paint. Once he finished his shower, he painted the walls, loving the way it looked like the ocean. He had yet to use the soaking tub but planned to soon, though he wished he had someone to share it with. Maybe someday, he thought as he rode over to Hannah's.

She was waiting outside when he pulled into her driveway. Damn, she looked good, dressed in her usual jeans and t-shirt, this time a white one that really complimented her sun kissed skin. She smiled as she got in his car, and he felt his heart flutter. What the hell was that all about?

"I'm so excited for tonight, just hope you aren't horrified by my singing."

"Same here, I'm a bass player, not a singer."

"I bet you'll be great."

He smiled and purposely started singing badly along with the radio. Hannah burst out laughing, a sound that he never tired of hearing. They stopped at the diner for dinner then headed over to the club. He saw Dean's truck when they arrived, so they headed inside and looked around until they saw Alex waving. There was a pitcher of beer and glasses waiting for them, so Mikael poured them each a glass. A little while later, the owner, Doug, came up on stage and announced the start of Karaoke. He spotted Hannah and called her up to stage.

"Ladies and gentlemen, you're in for a treat tonight as our favorite has joined us."

He handed Hannah the microphone.

"Thanks! For my first song, I'm going with a duet, but I will need someone to join me. Mikael, get your ass up here."

With Dean and Alex egging him on, Mikael joined her on stage. They flipped through the list of duets and decided on a love song, ironic with both of them being single and unlucky in that department. The music started, and Hannah began singing as the female part was first. Her voice was a mix of raspy and smoky, adding to her overall sexiness. Alex and Dean's jaws dropped as they'd never heart Hannah sing, and she was incredible. Mikael was even more surprised and couldn't believe that she thought she was lousy. They stood facing each other as they sang and the look they had on their faces fit the song perfectly.

"Look at them," Alex said to Dean. "They're in love."

"Are you sure?"

"I know that look anywhere. I don't think they know it yet, but wow, there's definite heat there."

"I hope so. They deserve each other."

They finished the song and received a standing ovation from the crowd. Mikael called Dean and Alex up there next then he and Hannah headed back to the table.

"Why did you tell me you were lousy?" Mikael asked.

"Because I am."

"No you're not. Your voice is amazing. I've been around a lot of singers during my career and you're one of the best I've ever heard."

"Yeah right."

Hearing her always doubt herself made Mikael mad. How could she not know how wonderful she is? Didn't anyone ever tell her? She could not have been more different than Liza, who always thought way more of herself than she should. He needed to find a way to convince Hannah how special she was.

Dean and Alex finished and made their way back to the table. Several more singers headed to the stage, but nobody came close to getting the reaction that Hannah and Mikael had. As the night was starting to wind down, Doug called Hannah and Mikael up for one last song. They picked an even more romantic song than the first time. As they sang, the love between them was even more apparent, though not to them. They finished to another standing ovation then handed the microphone to Doug, who announced the end of Karaoke for this week.

They headed back to the table and once they had polished off the pitcher, the four of them headed home.

"I had a great time tonight. Thanks for including me," Hannah said when they got back to her house

"Me too. We need to do that again."

"Any time."

She smiled and waved as she got out of the car and headed inside. Mikael felt that same flutter in his heart as when she smiled earlier. He headed home and right to bed, where he had a night filled with naughty dreams about Hannah. He woke up the next morning, soaking wet, his heart racing. He couldn't help but wonder what the fuck was going on. He knew he didn't want another relationship, but damn if this woman wasn't getting inside his head.

Chapter Six

It was mid-morning the day after their Karaoke outing. Hannah was upfront reviewing her inventory to see if she needed anything when Alex stopped by the shop. She had a shit-eatin' grin on her face, and Hannah wondered what was going on.

"Hey there, songbird," Alex said, laughing.

"Ha, ha, very funny."

"Seriously, girl, you're incredible. I had no idea you could sing like that."

"Well, thanks."

"Not to mention the heat between you and a certain bass player."

"What're you talking about?"

"You couldn't feel the heat between you and Mikael?"

"Are you drunk? We're just friends."

"It sure didn't look that way to me. Dean noticed it too. The way you two were looking at other when you were singing together was hot. It affected me and Dean so much that when we went home, well, you know."

"Damn, girl, you two fuck more than the hookers in the seedy part of town!"

"Funny. Seriously, though, I'm tellin' ya, Mikael likes you."

"Again, we're just friends. I would never be enough for him. Look at me."

"Stop it, you're gorgeous."

"Sure."

"Just think about it, okay, because I really think he's into you."

"Okay, I'll think about it."

"I gotta run, just wanted to stop in and be a nosy bitch, as usual."

Hannah laughed as they hugged goodbye. After Alex was gone, Hannah sat back down to finish the inventory but her mind kept wandering. What the hell was Alex talking about? There was nothing going on, just two friends making idiots out of themselves. There wasn't, nor would there ever be, anything more between her and Mikael. Then why can't I stop thinking about him, she thought to herself. She shook her head in an attempt to regain her focus and got the rest of her work done.

As noontime approached, the traffic into the store started picking up, as people tended to use their lunch hours to run errands. She was busy for about an hour or so then it slowed down again. Since she finished her inventory, she sat behind the counter, and let her mind wander. Was there something between her and Mikael? What did Alex and Dean see? Could it be possible that Mikael actually liked her? Did she have feelings for him? Her mind was a jumbled mess of emotions. She started daydreaming about what it might be like to actually be Mikael's girlfriend. She was so lost in thought, she never heard the door open and someone enter the store until his voice startled her.

"Hey there," Mikael said.

She didn't respond, so he snapped his fingers near her ear. She jumped a mile and gasped, as Mikael stood there doubled over in laughter. Her heart was pounding in her chest, but she couldn't be sure if it was because he scared or because of what Alex was saying earlier. Great, she thought, I'm going to drive myself crazy.

"Really fuckin' funny."

"I'm sorry," he said, still laughing.

"Yeah, you really sound like you are, jerk. You scared the shit out of me."

48

"I didn't mean too. What were you thinking about? You didn't hear me open the door, walk up to the counter or say hello."

"Just finishing up inventory to see if I needed to order anything, so I was pre-occupied."

"Any plans tonight?"

"Nope. I'm a real thrill-a-minute, huh?"

"Nothing wrong with a night in."

"It is if that's how you spend almost every night."

"I guess, but I always preferred quiet nights, though that is probably because of my ex-bitch."

Hannah smiled and he felt his heart do that damn flutter thing again. Damn, he wished he knew what the hell was causing that. And why did it seem to happen every time Hannah flashed that pretty smile?

"Where were you just now?" she asked, smiling again.

"Nowhere, just thinking."

"About?"

"Tonight. How about pizza, beer and a comedy movie marathon?"

"Sounds fun. Your place or mine?"

"I'd love to show you mine, since you showed me yours."

"Ummm," she said as she burst out laughing.

"Oh shit, I just realized what I said."

"It was hilarious! You okay with me bringing Cocoa?"

"Of course."

"I can grab the pizza and beer on the way."

"I already have beer, so just the pizza."

"Can't wait."

"Me either."

She smiled and there went that heart thing again. What the hell, he thought to himself. The last thing I thought I wanted was another relationship after Liza, but this woman is definitely having some sort of effect on me. He was able to shake it off for now, as he remembered the hell that Liza put him through. He needed to go clear his head before tonight.

"I'll let you get back to work. See you tonight."

"What time should I head over?"

"Around 6 work for you?"

"Absolutely."

He smiled and headed out. Hannah felt butterflies in the pit of her stomach as she watched him walk out. All she could think about was the conversation she had with Alex. Could she be starting to feel more than just friendship for him? She hoped not since there's no way a guy as hot as Mikael would want to be anything more than friends. She had a few more customers come in so she was able to stop thinking about it for now. Luckily the rest of the day was on the busier side, so her mind never wandered back to Mikael until she was on her way home.

She went in to grab a shower and the second she got in there, her mind went right to Mikael. She pictured him standing there with her, his hands on her naked, wet skin and her heart started doing flips inside her chest. She felt a heat starting to build between her thighs as she tried picturing him naked, which she took care of with a certain setting on her shower nozzle. After she got dressed and packed up a few things for Cocoa, she ordered the pizza and headed out.

It was a little after 6 when she got to his house. She almost crashed when she saw him sitting on his porch in jeans and a shirt that was only buttoned halfway up. She took a deep breath to try to calm herself before she got out of her car. She opened Cocoa's door and a big brown ball of fur flew of the car as she ran right up to Mikael. Hannah swore that dog was trying to tell her something, something which she needed to ignore. She grabbed the pizza and Cocoa's bag, and walked up to the porch. The pizza almost hit the ground when he flashed her a big smile.

"I thought we could eat outside, since it's nice out."

"Sounds good."

"Be right back."

While he was inside, she got Cocoa's dinner ready and set the bowl down on the porch. Mikael came back out with a couple paper plates and beers, and set them down on the table. Cocoa was just finishing up her last bite of food and let out a huge belch. Hannah laughed so hard, she snorted. She immediately turned bright red, mortified that she'd done that in front of Mikael.

"I'm sorry, that was disgusting of me."

"Not at all. I love when a woman isn't afraid to let loose and laugh."

"But the snort."

"It was cute."

She smiled, which had its usual effect on him. They each grabbed a slice of pizza and sat down to eat. They talked and laughed through the entire meal, as Mikael kept trying to make her snort again. He was successful quite a few times, but she no longer felt embarrassed by it. Once they were done, Mikael took everything inside while she waited on the porch. When he returned, she was putting Cocoa's harness on her.

"I just need to take Cocoa for her after-dinner walk, if you don't mind."

"Not at all. Mind if I join you?"

"Nope."

They walked down his driveway and started down the street, doing a lap around Mikael's neighborhood. His hand brushed hers a few times as they walked and each one sent a weird jolt through her body. She was having a hard time flighting her attraction to him, until her mom's words came floating back into her head. Her eyes filled with tears which she quickly tried to wipe away without Mikael seeing. If he noticed, he didn't say anything. When they got back to his house, Hannah asked where she could put the bag of Cocoa's business. He took it and threw it away for her and back came the butterflies. What the hell, she heard in her mom's voice, all he did was throw away a bag of your dog's shit and you get all crazy. Knock it the hell off.

As they walked inside, Mikael was wrestling with whether to ask why she started crying on the walk. He didn't want to embarrass her, but he was both curious and concerned that something was bothering his friend. He decided to hold off for now and see if she said anything.

"How about a tour before we start the marathon?"

"I'd love a tour."

He walked her around to each of the different rooms. When they got to his bedroom, he suddenly started imagining what it would be like to have her in his bed. He tried shaking off that image, but it seemed to be burned into his brain. When they got to the bathroom, her eyes went wide when she saw the tub.

"I bet it feels good to sit in there and relax," she said.

"I haven't actually done it yet."

"Really? You'd never get me out of there."

His heart started racing, as his brain replaced images of her in his bed to her in his tub. Of course, in both, she was naked in his arms. Hard as he tried, he just couldn't seem to shake those images of her. He hoped that once they sat down and started watching movies, that would help him get his mind out of the gutter. They headed back to the living and she sat down on the couch. He joined her, but made sure there was some space between them. He was afraid any kind of contact would send him into overload.

Mikael turned on the TV, brought up one of his streaming apps. Hannah saw her name on the screen as a watcher.

"How come my name's there?"

"I pulled some movies into that one that I thought you would like. That way, we could just let them keep playing until we were tired of watching."

"You're so sweet," she said, laughing.

Secretly, though, she truly was touched that he had put that much thought into it. Suddenly, her mom's voice popped in her head again, telling her to grow up and that him picking out some movies was nothing and that he would never want anything more than friendship with her. With that, the tears came back, but this time she couldn't keep them from spilling over. She hated that woman for the way she treated her for her entire childhood. Now, even with her mom completely cut out of her life physically, she was still always in her thoughts.

Mikael looked over when he heard her sniffle, and noticed her tears, like when they were walking Cocoa. This time, though, he couldn't ignore them. He moved closer to her and gently put a hand on her shoulder.

"What's wrong?"

"Nothing."

"Tears aren't nothing."

"They are in my case."

"Stop it. Tell me what's wrong."

"And wreck our friendship? No."

"Why would you think that?"

"Because I'm ridiculous and I need to grow up."

"Talk to me, please, I'm your friend."

"But I've never told anyone this."

"Then you need to let it out. It helped me so much when I told you the full story about Liza. Let me help you the same way."

She knew he was right. She had to do this, but damn reliving this was going to hurt. She took a deep breath before she started talking.

"My mother was built a lot like Liza, but I took after my dad's side of the family. My mom never let me forget that men would never want a woman who was built like me. Men only like those skinny girls like Liza and like my mom. That's why I started hanging around where all the rock guys did. They didn't care that I was ugly, they slept with me anyway. But that stopped being enough. I wanted a relationship, but I know that's never going to be in the cards for me. I stopped speaking to my mom as soon as I was able to move out on my own."

"She was dead wrong. Not all men like those type of women."

"That's what I found out. She actually hated me because my dad left her for a woman who looked like the way I turned out looking, which made her hate me even more. Despite leaving her behind, I've never been able to forget what she said to me."

"I love those sexy curves."

"You're just trying to get to stop crying."

"No. I really mean it. You're hotter than hell."

"I'm sorry. I just can't. Friends is it."

"I know you have feelings for me."

"I just can't. I'm not good enough for you."

"But Hannah, I..."

She cut him off before he could finish. "Friends, please."

"You need to put this behind you."

"I wish I could. Who knows, maybe if I'd had the chance to tell her what she did to me, but I just ended up leaving instead."

"Maybe you could look her up."

"Forget it. It's just not in the cards for me to ever find love."

He gave in for now, but he wasn't done. He had to figure out a way to make her believe his feelings were real and that she was a beautiful, amazing woman. He knew it was going to take something over the top, but he knew he could do it.

"How about we drown our sorrows with a couple movies then."

"Sure."

He started the first movie he had picked. After a few minutes, he realized his hand was still on her shoulder, so he slid it across to her other shoulder and gave her a light hug. He felt her lay her head on his shoulder and looked over at her. His heart nearly burst out of chest as he realized somewhere along the way, he had fallen for her. He could definitely get used to snuggling on the couch, or anywhere else she wanted, with this beautiful woman.

Before Hannah even realized what she doing, she had laid her head on his shoulder. She thought about apologizing and moving it, but something felt so right, sitting here, snuggling with him. Was it possible that he truly did like her? No way, her mom's voice told her. She was able to silence that voice for now and focus on the movie but she knew she would pay for that later.

Partway through the second movie, Mikael heard soft snoring. He looked over and Hannah was sound asleep on his shoulder. By the end of the movie, she was still sound asleep, so he slowly got up and laid her down on the couch, then covered her with a blanket. After a soft kiss on the top of her head, he took Cocoa out for a last bathroom break, then headed off to bed himself.

Chapter Seven

The sound of Cocoa barking jarred Hannah out of her slumber. She sat up and looked around, confused for a minute about where she was until she realized it was Mikael's house. Once the fog in her brain cleared, she recalled that she only saw one full movie and part of another. She hoped like hell she didn't snore or do anything else embarrassing in her sleep. Since the only one to ever share her bed was Cocoa, she had no way of knowing what she did in her sleep. She saw part of a pot of coffee and figured Mikael must be awake, but she didn't see him. Cocoa barked at the front door, so Hannah looked outside and saw him sitting on the porch. She opened the door and let him know she was awake.

"I'm so sorry for falling asleep."

"No need to be."

"I hope I didn't do anything embarrassing."

"Not at all. You were snoring quietly, that's it."

"That's embarrassing."

"I thought it was cute."

She rolled her eyes. He was being way too nice to her. She looked at her watch and was relieved that she would still have time to shower and change before she had to open the store.

"Would you like some coffee and breakfast?"

"I don't want to be any trouble."

"You won't. I enjoy cooking."

"Okay."

"Any requests?"

"Nope, not picky."

"Cool. Help yourself to some coffee."

"Thanks."

He loved that she was willing to do things for herself. If he had said that to Liza, she would have stomped her foot and made him do it. He was so glad to be away from that bitch. Between the way Liza had treated him and the way Hannah's mom had treated her, it almost made sense that they were put into each other's life. A few minutes later, Mikael served her the most delicious omelet she'd ever eaten.

"Wow, so good," she said between bites.

"Thank you."

After she ate, she insisted on cleaning up since he had cooked. When she was done, she gathered up Cocoa's stuff and got ready to head home.

"Thanks for everything last night. Sorry again about falling asleep."

"You're welcome. Can I see you tonight?"

"I think we better take it easy."

"Why?"

"I don't want anything to jeopardize our friendship."

"What if I want to be more than friends?"

"Stop it, look at me. My mother was right about me."

"The fuck she was. Why won't you believe me?"

"I have a mirror."

"Then use it. You're beautiful."

"Sure."

"I'm going to find a way to prove it to you."

"Good luck with that. Listen, I gotta run if I want to get the store open on time."

As she headed out to her car, he watched her walk, hips swaying so sexily that he felt his dick starting to stir in his jeans. Fuck, he wanted that woman. Now, he had to figure out how to convince her. He sat down on the porch and a plan started to formulate in his mind. Hannah would never be able to say no to this. He couldn't wait to put his plan into action today. If everything worked out, he could have the woman of his dreams in his arms tonight. He got inside and Leo came over to sit with him. Looking in his boy's handsome face, he told him his plan. Leo just looked at him, probably more interested in food than what Mikael was saying.

After showering and changing, Hannah was able to make it to the store a little before her regular open time. She was experiencing one of the slowest days she'd had in a while. Probably for the best, as she was having a hard time concentrating on anything other than Mikael. She didn't expect she'd ever see or hear from again after what she told him. He probably thought about it after she left and realized her mother was right. She felt her eyes fill with tears but was able to keep them from spilling over, a relief as she heard the shop door open a minute later.

Customers started to stream in a little more steadily through midafternoon then stopped. She still had about two hours left before closing. She decided to check out her social media feed to see what was new and of course went right to Mikael's page. She noticed that he had changed his relationship status to single and had removed any references to Liza, including pictures. She had to admit that made her a little happier than she would have thought. She sighed audibly, sad that even with him now being single, he would still never be hers.

Hannah was just finishing straightening up a couple of shelves when she heard the door open.

"I'm getting ready to close," she called out.

She walked up to the front and her jaw dropped. She was standing face to face with the woman who treated her like shit her entire life. Her heart started racing, a combination of butterflies and anger filling her stomach. Being a constant voice in her head wasn't enough, now she was here to hurl more insults in person.

"Hi, Hannah," she said quietly.

"Mom, what are you doing here?"

"It's been a long time."

"Not long enough."

"Is that any way to speak to your mother?"

"What about the way you spoke to me all my life? I never did anything to deserve that."

"I was damn well justified. Your father left me for a woman built a lot like you are now."

"And?"

"I grew to hate women that looked like that."

"But I'm your daughter."

"Unfortunately."

"Why did you even come here? Just to remind me that you never cared."

"I just wanted to see if you'd finally become someone I could be proud of, but clearly you haven't."

"Really? I run a successful business, which I recently expanded to also include a booth at the farmers market and I own my home. Most parents would be proud of that."

"Like that matters. I thought you would have gotten some work done to remove all those curves."

"So, looks are all that matters? You know what, you're a terrible excuse for a mother."

"And you're a horribly unattractive excuse for a daughter."

"The fuck she is."

Hannah turned around and saw Mikael standing there, a scowl on his face at what he just heard.

"And who are you?" Hannah's mom demanded.

"I'm Mikael, your beautiful, sexy, amazing daughter's friend."

"You clearly need your eyes checked, young man. Men do not like women who look my daughter."

Unable to stand being near her mother for one more minute, Hannah started to walk away, She just couldn't deal with this anymore. After a couple steps, she stopped and turned back around, again facing her.

"GO TO HELL."

"Excuse me."

"All my life, you did nothing but put me down. Your cruelty has done nothing but negatively impact my life. Even when men have shown interest in me, I've always pushed them away. Your voice has never left my head. All I ever hear is more of your insults and I'm sick and fucking tired of feeling this way. I've waited a long time to be able to say all this to you. It feels like a weight has been lifted off my shoulders and I can finally move on. I hope you have a wonderful rest of your life. Now get out. Out of my store and out of my life."

Her mom opened her mouth to say something, but Hannah put her hand up.

"Don't. There's nothing more I ever want to hear from you. Don't ever come here again."

"Fine, but before I go, I came here to tell you that your father died," she said as she turned on her heel and headed for the door.

After her mom stormed out, Hannah sank to the floor, her body shaking as she sobbed. Mikael sat down next to her and held her tightly, letting her cry into his shoulder.

"I'm so sorry about your father, but I'm proud of you," he said softly.

"Thanks. You've been such a great friend."

Mikael's heart sank a little, but he didn't want to push anything tonight. So, he just sat and held her. After about an hour, she finally started to calm down. She got up and started to head back to her office. She had just been getting ready to close when her mom came in, so she still had to count the till and get the money locked up in her safe. Mikael walked with her, sitting quietly in her office while she finished up, then walked her out to her car.

"Thanks for helping me. But, how did you know?"

"I didn't. I came to convince you to come over tonight and I saw you."

'I appreciate it, but I really just need to go home tonight."

"I understand."

She smiled as she got in her car after letting Cocoa get in the back-seat and headed home. Mikael wanted to follow her, but he also wanted to give her some space, so he headed home. He really needed to figure out a way to convince her to trust him with her heart. He hoped that the confrontation with her mom would finally free her from her mom's voice and allow to believe how beautiful she is.

He was feeling restless, so he decided to head to the club. When he got inside, he saw Dean at the bar, so he took the stool next to him.

"No Alex?"

"She's with the girls tonight. Hey, you okay, man?"

"I guess."

"Woman trouble?"

"Yeah. Dude, I'm in love with Hannah."

"Failing to see the problem."

"She won't give me anything more than friendship."

"Has she said why?"

He told Dean the whole story about Hannah's mom, including what he witnessed earlier.

"She sounds awful. Poor Hannah."

"Yeah, total bitch. I was so proud of Hannah for finally telling her off."

"Maybe that will help. But dude, give her time."

"I don't know how much more I can take."

"Trust me. I didn't push Alex too hard and look at us now."

"I'll try."

"Just keep doing things as a friend, and give her time to realize how she feels."

"Thanks, man."

After a couple beers, they headed out. Mikael wished he was going home to Hannah the way Dean was to Alex. He drove past Hannah's house and saw that all the lights were off. He hoped she was getting the rest she needed. He headed home, but was still feeling restless, so he grabbed one of his basses and started strumming. He pictured himself playing for Hannah. He loved this woman more than he'd ever loved anyone, and he wanted nothing more than to hold her, kiss her, make love to her.

After he was done playing, he headed to bed. He woke up the next morning, heart racing after the dream he had about Hannah. He dreamed that he had gone to the shop just like he had last night, but instead of pushing him away again, Hannah let him take her home. She gave into her feelings and they spent the night in his bed, passionately making love. He got up, showered and dressed then had some breakfast.

When it was approaching lunch time, he stopped at Hannah's favorite pizza place and grabbed a pie for her and Kurt. He parked out back next to Hannah and headed inside. The store wasn't too busy at that time, so they had time to eat. Hannah felt something in her stomach. It was an odd mix of butterflies and sensations, better known as love. She had felt her feelings for Mikael changing, but she just couldn't bring herself to give in. Things were starting to pick up, so Mikael cleaned up from lunch.

"Thanks for bringing lunch in," Hannah said.

"My pleasure."

"Could we maybe hang out tonight?"

"Sure. What'd you have in mind?"

"A takeout and movie night. I promise I won't tall asleep tonight."

"Sounds good."

"Text me what you want and I'll grab the food on my way."

"Sounds good."

Mikael headed out, making a stop at the beer distributor and grabbing her favorite wine coolers. He also stopped to get a bouquet of her favorite flowers. Even though this wasn't an official date, he still wanted to make it feel special for her. When he got home, he queued up some comedies for them to watch. He loved the sound of Hannah's laugh, especially when she did that cute snort. Mikael texted her, asking if Chinese food was cool for dinner. She agreed, so he sent her his order.

The rest of the afternoon was busy and flew by. When it was closing time, Hannah changed the sign and locked the door. She and Kurt walked the store doing any straightening and cleaning anything that needed. When they were done, Kurt headed home while Hannah went to her office for her nightly task. After she had the money secured, she called the local Chinese takeout restaurant then headed out. She saw a man walking around the parking lot. She got an odd feeling that she knew him, but he didn't look at all familiar, so she shook it off and got in her car.

After picking up the food, she drove to Mikael's house. Something was still nagging her about the man she saw, but she quickly put that out of her head. All she wanted was a fun, relaxing night with her friend. She got Cocoa out of the car, and was about to get the food out when she saw the door open. Mikael came down and helped her carry everything in. They unpacked the food and each made themselves a plate, then headed into the living room to start movie night while they ate.

They ended up watching all three parts of The Hangover trilogy, one of Hannah's favorites. She started feeling sleepy so decided she ought to get going, as she had work in the morning.

"Thanks for tonight. This was exactly what I needed."

"Anytime, beautiful."

Hannah blushed and smiled, but for the first time, didn't deny his compliment or down herself. Maybe confronting her mom really did help her get some closure and some freedom from her hellish childhood. He walked her out to her car. It took every ounce of self-control not to grab her and kiss her. Instead he waved as she pulled out. He wasn't sure how much longer he'd be able to resist her and he knew he needed to do something.

Chapter Eight

Hannah was a little rattled when she arrived at the shop the next morning. She was still processing the emotions of confronting her mother, along with her changing feelings for Mikael. She knew deep down she was falling in love with Mikael, despite her best efforts to fight it. Now that her mom's voice was gone from her brain, there was nothing keeping her from him. Nothing except for her own stupid fears. He had told her time and again that she was beautiful, but she just couldn't make herself believe him.

Kurt arrived not long after she did, two coffees and a bag of Danish in his hand. He handed a coffee to Hannah and put the bag on the counter. Hannah thanked him and filled him in on her mom's visit. Kurt gave her a big hug and told her he was proud of her for finally getting that closure she needed. She was so grateful to have him as an employee, and more importantly, as a friend. She peeked in the bag and saw her favorite, cheese danish.

As lunchtime approached, Hannah looked for Mikael to come through the door but no sign of him. He must have given up on me, she thought, feeling a bit sad. She asked Kurt what he wanted and had food delivered. Unlike the day before, today was really slow in the afternoon. Kurt headed out early as he had a date planned. Hannah felt a little pang, wishing she herself had a date. She knew it was nobody's fault but her own.

With things being so slow, she walked the store and did her cleaning early. Once she was done, she checked her inventory order and added a few things. All her work done, she grabbed the latest trashy novel she was reading out of her purse and picked up where she had left off. With every naughty scene she read, she pictured her and Mikael acting it out. At this rate, she was going to have to get Vinny the Vibrator out when she got home. She only had one more customer the rest of the afternoon, and ended up finishing her book.

She took another walk around the store, straightening shelves and making sure nothing else needed cleaning. Once she was happy with how everything looked, she went back up front and waited in case anyone else came in. She saw Eden leaving her place for the day and waved. Eden's business had been picking up, which made her happy. She loved seeing other women achieve success just as she had. Closing time was finally only five minutes away, so she started getting things ready. She locked the door so nobody else could enter and was getting ready to count out her cash register, when the phone rang.

"I'm closed," she yelled at the phone. "Rock the Fur, this is Hannah. Can I help you?"

She heard a male voice on the other end, a voice that brought those butterflies back in full force. Mikael.

"I'm sorry to call when I know you're closing. I thought I had another bag of kitty litter, but I was wrong. Is there any chance you could stay open for a few extra minutes?"

"If it would help, I would be happy to drop some off."

"That would be great. Thanks."

"I just need to get my till counted and ready for the morning then lock up. Be there soon."

"Can't wait."

As she got the bags he asked for, she couldn't help but wonder what he meant when he said can't wait. Surely, he couldn't be that desperate for kitty litter, so what was he up to? She couldn't worry about that now. Besides, whatever it was, the answer was no. She knew he couldn't really like her or be attracted to her in any way. By the time she arrived in his driveway, her heart was beating out of her chest, as she was still trying to get over her attraction to him. She grabbed the bags, walked to his door, and rang the doorbell. When he opened the door, she almost dropped the bags. He was standing there in nothing but a pair of shorts. She couldn't take her eyes off his sexy chest, well except when they took a peek at his bulge. He took the bags from her, so she turned to leave.

"Where do you think you're going?"

"Home."

"How can I repay you?"

"I can think of something."

The minute the words came out of her mouth, she regretted it. She knew he would surely tell her to get the hell off his property. Mikael's eyebrows raised but he didn't respond. Instead, he moved aside and motioned her in.

"I can't. Cocoa's in the car."

He walked over to her car, grabbed Cocoa's leash and brought her in, so Hannah followed. He sure was pushy, she thought to herself, but she found that she actually liked that. He touched her arm as they walked inside, and she felt electricity shoot through her body. He put the bags down and escorted her to the living room. She couldn't get over seeing him in just shorts. He never showed much in his pictures, so she often tried to imagine what he looked like. Even her dirty imagination hadn't done him justice.

"Have a seat," he said, pointing at the couch.

"Thanks."

He sat down next to her and said, "So, you said you could think of a way I could repay you. Well, let's hear it," he said naughtily.

"I just meant you could pay for the kitty litter. A plain girl like me could never expect anything in return."

"You're as far from plain as I've ever seen."

"Yeah right."

"You are so damn hot and sexy."

Before she could respond, he leaned in and pressed his lips to hers. She felt his tongue eagerly exploring her mouth and she lost all control.

She intertwined her tongue with his, feeling sensations travel through her like nothing she'd ever felt before. He grabbed the stereo remote and put some music on.

"Dance with me."

He stood and held out his hand. Hannah put her hand in his and stood. He walked her to the middle of the living room and took her into his arms, just as he'd done at the wedding. She let her body melt into his. The feeling of his strong arms around her combined with his body heat and sexy cologne had her on sensory overload. He kissed her even more eagerly as they danced. She lost all control of her mind, as her body took over. That is, until she heard her mother's voice telling her how men would never want her, and she pulled away.

"What's wrong?"

"I can't do this."

"Why not?"

"Look at me. No, wait, don't look at me. I'm hideous."

"You're beautiful."

She pulled away, shaking her head, as tears spilled out of her beautiful eyes.

"But my mother..."

"To hell with her. She's dead wrong about you."

"No, she wasn't."

"What happened to the confidence you got after finally telling her how you felt?"

"I had time to think about it, and I realized she was right about me all along.

"Stop! You're stunning and I'm damn well going to prove it to you."

He took her hand and walked her to his bedroom. He stopped outside the door and kissed her tenderly.

"Only if you want to," he said softly.

Something in his eyes made her respond, "I want to."

He walked her inside and again wrapped her in his arms, kissing her. This kiss was different. More eager, more passionate, than any he'd given her so far. The closeness of their bodies allowed her to feel the erection growing inside his shorts, and she felt herself getting wet.

Before her brain could stop her, her mouth whispered, "I want you."

"I want you too."

Mikael slipped his hands under her shirt, softly caressing her skin as he lifted her shirt off. Fuck, she was stunning. He removed her bra, and while she blushed, she didn't try to stop him. He felt her breathing become rapid as he gently flicked his tongue on her hard nipple. He had wondered on many an occasion what her naked chest would look like, and he hadn't come close. She was breathtakingly beautiful.

He felt her soft hands running all over his already exposed chest. He pulled her in close, loving the feeling of her skin touching his. He kissed her passionately, his tongue dancing with hers inside her mouth. She moaned softly into his mouth as he moved his hands down to her soft bottom. He couldn't get enough of her, and he really needed to be inside her. He opened her jeans and slid his hand inside her panties. He almost shot his load right there in his shorts when he felt her shaved mound.

He slid her jeans and her panties down to the floor and she stepped out of them. He looked her up and down, completely mesmerized by her sexy curves. She refused to look up and make eye contact with him, so he put his hand under her chin and gently lifted her head. Her cheeks were dark crimson, and she tried to look away, but he stopped her.

"You're the most stunning woman I've ever seen."

"How is that possible after Liza was your girlfriend?"

"Not all men like women that look like her."

"Nobody's ever told me that before."

"Then they're fuckin' morons and their loss is my gain."

She smiled at his words, and for the first time in as far back as she could remember, she felt comfortable with a man. That comfort turned into confidence and she put her hands on the waistband of his shorts, tugging on them until they were around his ankles. She was delighted to find out that he wasn't wearing any underwear. She looked him up and down, her eyes wide at the size of his dick. Her pussy started throbbing with desire, aching to feel him inside her.

She walked over to his bed and laid down, wagging her finger for him to join her. He laid down next to her and pulled her close.

"Are ya sure you want me or would you prefer what I saw Cocoa with that day at your shop?"

Laughing, she responded, "Dickhead!"

"Such a dirty mouth."

"Well, I'm a dirty girl."

"Prove it!"

Gazing into his eyes, she got on all fours and wrapped her sexy plump lips around his cock, sucking hard as she ran her tongue up and down his shaft. He tasted so damn good that she started sucking even harder, as he groaned with pleasure. She almost forgot what it was like to be a actual person, and it was incredible.

Mikael couldn't take his eyes off her as she pleasured him. It had been far too long since a woman had gone anywhere near his cock. He was definitely glad it was this woman, this beautiful, amazing woman, who had her lips wrapped around his dick. The harder she sucked, the louder he started groaning. Feeling like he was close to coming, he stopped her.

"I need my dick inside that pussy now."

She rolled onto her back, opening her legs wide for him. He was awestruck by her beauty. His eyes couldn't get enough of this amazing woman lying there, completely naked, waiting for him to be inside her. He moved on top of her and slowly thrust his dick inside her. Fuck, she was so wet and so warm. Her sweet pussy felt like heaven wrapped around him as he slowly slid in and out of her. He had imagined so many times what it would feel like to be inside her. This was so much better than anything he'd dreamed up.

"Oh, Mikael, so good."

She could feel the pressure building inside her as he slowly slid every delicious inch of himself in and out of her, their bodies in perfect sync. He held her close, kissing her as they continued their incredible dance until they took flight in a universe of intense pleasure. They moaned in unison as he filled her pussy with his cream while she exploded in an orgasm so incredible, she could see the most beautiful colors she'd even seen.

As they laid in each others' arms, basking in the afterglow of the most incredible sex they'd ever had, she looked up at Mikael with a silly smile on her face.

"Wow, you must really like kitty litter," she said, laughing.

As he laughed, he kissed her tenderly before they drifted off to a blissful night's sleep.

Chapter Nine

Hannah woke up the next morning with a pair of strong sexy arms still wrapped around her. She felt him stir behind her, both of them still naked after their night of passion. Part of her felt like it must have been a dream, but it wasn't. She was actually here, in his house, in his bed, in his arms. She rolled over so she was facing him and kissed him softly on those sexy lips of his. He pulled her closer to him and she could feel him getting hard. Having awakened that naughty side of her, she reached her hand down and started stroking his cock.

"Mmm, good baby," he said sleepily.

"I want you."

He was wide awake now. He pulled her on top of him, taking in every last beautiful curve as he felt her pussy wrap around his dick. She slowly slid up and down his shaft, and fuck, she felt amazing. He moved his hands to that sexy round ass of hers, squeezing hard as she moaned. He loved watching her beautiful breasts bouncing as she fucked him. Who knew that something as dull as kitty litter would have led to the most incredible sex he'd ever had?

She started moaning louder as she moved closer to exploding around him. He rubbed her clit with his fingers as she rode him, quickly sending her over the edge. She threw her head back, moaning as she experienced an earth-shattering orgasm. She looked so damn hot that he quickly followed with an explosion of his own, filling her with his hot cream. She collapsed down on his chest and kissed him, his arms holding her tight.

Gazing into her beautiful eyes, he said, "I love you."

"I love you."

Hearing her say those words made his heart start racing. How had he gotten so lucky to find this woman? Nothing had ever felt more right than being here, skin on skin with the most beautiful woman he'd ever laid eyes on. She moved next to him and snuggled in close, her head on his chest. She sighed softly, her warm breath sending a jolt though his body. Any touch from this woman drove him wild. For the first time in his life, he felt like he was truly in love and damn did it feel good.

"I wanna fuck again, my sexy bass god," she purred.

"You're a very naughty woman."

"I'm sorry."

"Don't be. I love it. What else do you like in bed?"

"I could never tell you that!"

"Babe, I'm pretty sure you can tell me anything after what we did."

"I'm afraid you'll judge me."

"I won't. I might even like it."

She took a deep breath and replied, "I always wanted to try role-play in the bedroom."

"Me too."

"Seriously?"

"I swear. I just never did because I never found a woman that wanted to."

"Well, now you have."

"Just you wait, baby."

"Ooh, what do you have in mind?"

"You'll find in due time, my dirty woman," he teased

Hannah smiled as she looked up at him and kissed him. She would love to have stayed in bed longer, but she needed to get home and get ready to open the store. She tried to get up but Mikael wouldn't let go of her. She tickled his belly until he was laughing hysterically and finally released her from his arms. He felt like himself again and it felt amazing.

"Do you really have to go?"

"I need to shower and change before I head to the store."

"You could shower here."

"I would if I had clothes to change into."

"Maybe you could keep a couple outfits here."

"Okay. Next time I come over, I'll bring a couple with me."

"Why not tonight?"

"You aren't sick of me?"

"No way. I would love if you and Cocoa spent the night again."

"I'd love to."

"We're gonna have fun. Now, though, do you have time for breakfast?"

"Not if I want to open on time."

"Damn. But we'll make up for it later."

"Mmmm, so excited."

She and Cocoa headed home and the second she walked out the door, Mikael found himself missing her. This was such a welcome change from Liza, a woman he wished would never come home. Now that Hannah told him about liking role-play, he had a plan for tonight and just had to grab a few things. He headed out figuring once he was done, he would see if she could take a lunch break in the park.

After he finished his naughty shopping trip, he stopped and grabbed lunch then headed over to the pet shop. The store was empty other than Hannah and Kurt, when he walked in. He saw her face light up when she saw him, and his heart skipped a beat. Damn, he loved this woman. He walked over to her, grabbed her and kissed her.

"Can you take a lunch break?"

She turned to Kurt and asked, "Are you okay to handle the store for a little bit?"

"Yes, go enjoy lunch," he replied.

"Thanks." She turned back to Mikael, and said, "Let's go."

"How about the park?" he asked.

"I love the park."

They held hands as they walked over, and walked the path until they found an open picnic table and sat down. Mikael took the sandwiches and iced teas out of the bag and handed her one. After they finished eating, they walked to one of the open benches and sat down. He put his arm around her and turned her head toward his, caressing her sexy lips with his. They sat on the bench kissing until they heard a couple of throats clear. There stood Dean and Alex with amused looks on their faces.

"Well, well, well, what do we have here?" Dean teased.

"Shut it, asshole," Mikael replied.

"Seriously, are you two together?"

"Nooooo," Hannah sniped. "Mikael tripped and his lips collided with mine."

Everyone laughed as Mikael pulled her close and kissed her head. He loved that sassy side of her, and he knew for sure she was going to love what he planned for her tonight.

"Sorry, but you set yourself up for that," she said to Dean.

"You're right," he lamented.

Alex smiled and added, "I'm so happy for you. Both of you deserve this. We'll leave you be, so you can get back to smoochin'."

Dean made kissing noises as he and Alex continued their walk. Mikael and Hannah went back to playing a hot game of tonsil hockey until they were both out of breath. When they finally came up for air, Hannah looked at her watch and realized they'd been at the park for almost an hour.

"I better get back in case things pick up. I don't want poor Kurt having to deal with a crowd alone."

"Okay, I'll walk you back."

Things had just started to pick up when they got back, so Hannah thanked Mikael for lunch then started helping customers out in the store while Kurt took care of the cash register. Mikael stood for a few minutes watching her work, loving the sight of those sexy curves in action before he headed home. He couldn't wait to get her naked later. He made one last stop at the grocery store to get what he needed for dinner. He really wanted this to be a special night for his woman.

The shop was busy for the rest of the day, so time flew by. Hannah was glad as she was really looking forward to her night with her new man. Since Mikael first made love to her, she hadn't heard her mom's voice again and she liked the freedom, hoping it would last. She stopped home and packed up some stuff for her and Cocoa so she didn't have to rush home in the morning. Her heart was racing just from thinking about being in Mikael's arms. She sped over to his house, smiling when she saw him sitting on the porch with a bouquet of flowers in his hand.

He took her bags and handed her the flowers. She smiled sweetly then surprised him by giving him a smack on his sexy ass. He loved this naughty side of her and he was so lucky she was willing to bring it out for him. She was so quiet when he first met her, but something had definitely awakened that dirty girl she was hiding and he loved it. Shit, he loved her. He couldn't wait for her to see what he had in store for her after dinner.

"Something smells delicious," she said when they got inside.

"I made lasagna."

"Yum, one of my favorites."

"Oh good. Italian is one of my favorites, both to eat and cook."

"Mine too."

"Can I pour you a glass of wine?'

"I'd love some."

"Do you have a favorite? I have plenty of choices."

"Moscato is my favorite."

"Coming right up."

"I hope that's not the only thing coming tonight."

"Damn, naughty woman."

"You ain't seen nothin' yet!"

Hearing her say that got his dick stirring but he talked himself down as he had plans for her later. He poured them each a glass of wine then brought the salad and garlic bread to the table. He cut two pieces of lasagna and carried them over as well. Everything looked so delicious, she didn't know what to try first. Not as delicious, of course, as the man who prepared it, but she would get to taste him later. After they finished eating, and cleaning up, Mikael excused himself to his bedroom. He came back out a few minutes later wearing only a white lab coat and carrying a medical bag.

Hannah's mouth started watering when she saw him, and that wasn't the only part of her that got wet.

"Dr. Love at your service," he said with a naughty wink.

"I didn't call for a doctor."

"I heard you had a fever between those sexy legs. I'm just the one to provide some relief."

"Oooh, doctor. Now that you mention it, I think I may need a full body exam."

"Right this way," he said, pointing toward his bedroom.

Hannah practically ran down the hall, she was so excited. Mikael followed close behind, laughing at how eager she was.

"Disrobe and lay that sexy body down on the bed."

"Yes, doctor."

She slowly stripped her clothes off as Mikael sat there licking his lips. When she was done, she laid down on the bed.

"Open wide. And I don't mean your mouth."

She spread her legs wide, as Mikael walked over to the bed. He got on his knees and ran his hands up her legs, sending chills through her entire body. She felt his tongue start teasing her clit as she arched her back and moaned. Damn, she tasted so good. He starting licking harder while sliding a couple fingers inside her. She moaned louder as he brought her closer and closer to orgasm.

"Suck on my clit. Oh, fuck."

He sucked her as he fucked her pussy with his fingers until her entire body started shaking. She screamed, her entire body quivering in ecstasy.

"It feels like you still have a bit of a fever, so I need to do another test."

"Mmmm."

"This one requires my tool."

"Yes, please, doctor."

He climbed on top of her and slid his hard, throbbing cock deep inside her. A deep growl escaped her lips as she raked her long purple fingernails down his back. She moved them down to his sexy ass, and grabbed it, trying to get him even deeper. He felt so damn good inside her. She ground her hips against him while he fucked her hard and fast. His breathing shallowed and she felt warm cream fill her pussy. He laid down next to her and pulled her close, kissing her hard.

"I think you're cured now, babe."

"I'm still feeling a bit feverish. I think I need a few more tests done."

"We can't have that. Maybe we should test your mouth this time."

She straddled him and lowered her head, wrapping her lips around his dick. She took every last inch inside her mouth without even the slightest gag, running her tongue up and down his shaft with each stroke. He sounded like a lion, loving the feeling of those sexy lips sucking his cock. He felt himself getting close to exploding.

"Fuck, I'm about to come."

She removed her mouth from his dick and said, "I wanna drink you."

Taking him back inside her mouth, he quickly shot his load right down her throat. She locked eyes with him, swallowed and licked her lips. It was the hottest thing he'd seen her do yet and he was hard again. Looking down at that delicious cock, she slid up his body and took his erection deep inside her, riding him hard and fast until they both climaxed in simultaneous earth-shattering explosions of passion.

"Mmm, doctor, that's what I call really good bedside manner!"

Chapter Ten

F riday was especially busy. This time of year tended to bring travelers looking for a weekend getaway, and the uniqueness of her shop always drew tourists. The weather today was sunny and unseasonably warm, which brought her even more customers. She and Kurt barely had a chance to take a bathroom break all day. Mikael dropped lunch off for them, but didn't hang around due to the steady stream of people coming in and out.

He was excited about tonight. This would be his first time spending the night at Hannah's house, and all he could think about was being naked in her bed. They planned on a pizza and movie night. He was hoping they would make an early exit to the bedroom. He pulled into her driveway a few minutes before he expected her home and waited on her porch. He saw a huge smile appear on her weary face when she saw him. Every time he saw that smile, his heart danced in his chest.

"Hey there, beautiful," he said when she reached her porch.

Amidst a huge yawn, she responded, "Mmmm, hey, sexy."

He took her keys and opened her door. They were greeted by a brown ball of fur. Mikael waited for Cocoa to take care of her business so Hannah could go in and sit. Mikael grabbed his overnight bag and his guitar case off her porch and walked inside, Cocoa right on his heels. He ordered dinner while Hannah got Cocoa's ready. While Cocoa ate, Hannah walked to her bedroom to take her shoes off.

"How about we go right to comfy clothes tonight?" Mikael suggested.

"Sounds like exactly what the doctor ordered," she said with a wink.

"Anytime you feel that fever again, you let me know."

"You can count on that, Dr. Love."

Mikael watched as she removed her clothes, unable to peel his eyes away from her beautiful skin. She put her jammies on, and all he could think about was getting them back off later. After he finished changing, they headed back to the living room and waited for the pizza to arrive. When they heard the doorbell, Mikael made her stay on the couch and relax while he took care of everything.

"You don't have to do that," she said. "I'm not like Liza."

"I can see how tired you are. I want to do this. Trust me, it's not the same thing. You never demand anything of me, so I'm happy to help when needed."

"Thank you."

"My pleasure."

"It will be later," she purred.

"Damn, woman!"

Hannah turned on Netflix and they decided on a movie. Once they finished eating, Mikael put an arm around his sexy woman as she laid her head on his shoulder. She made it through one movie and half of a second before she was sound asleep on Mikael's shoulder. He gently laid her head down in his lap and covered her with a blanket. Looking down at where her head was filled his brain with all kinds of naughty thoughts. She stirred about an hour later.

"Mmm, while my head's down here, is there anything that needs sucked?"

"Woman!"

She slipped her hand into his pants, stroking his cock. Feeling his erection, she said, "Oh, someone wants to come out and play."

She got up and stood in front of him. He felt her tugging on his waistband, so he lifted his hot ass off the couch. She slid his pants down to his ankles, got on her knees and wrapped her soft lips around his dick.

"Oh, woman, so hot," he groaned.

After a little more hot action from her sexy mouth, she stood and removed her pajama bottoms. Straddling him, she slid her pussy down his cock. He slid in easily her pussy was so wet. He supported her hips with his hands as she rode him hard and fast. She felt him empty himself inside her as her pussy exploded around him. She collapsed against his chest, her sweat-dampened hair spilling over his face. He kissed her hard, holding her tight.

"I love you, woman."

"Mmm, I love you too. Will you play for me?"

"My bass?"

"No, your ass. Yes, of course, your bass, silly."

"I'm not sure little miss sassypants deserves to see me play."

Giving him her best puppy-dog eyes, she begged, "Please, play for me. I wanna watch those sexy fingers stroking your instrument."

"No way I can say no now, dirty girl."

He got dressed and walked to her bedroom to grab the guitar he brought with him. He sat back down on the couch and started playing for her. She had always preferred the deeper bass sound, and was mesmerized watching him play. All she could think about was what he'd done to her with those magic fingers. He played for a little while, until his music soothed his wild woman to sleep. After taking Cocoa out for a bathroom break, he carried Hannah to her bedroom, laid her down and climbed in next to her. He pulled her close, gave her a soft kiss on the forehead then quickly feel asleep next to her.

They woke up Saturday, elated that the weekend had finally arrived, and just their luck, after a gorgeous week of sunny, comfortable days, it was chilly and raining. For the first time since they got together, Mikael had spent the night at Hannah's house. They enjoyed some extra sleep then had a nice brunch and now were back in bed snuggled under a blanket. He still couldn't believe this beautiful woman was his and that she actually enjoyed being with him. He gently caressed her cheek, as she gazed at him. He could feel the strength of her love for him just by the look in her eyes, as he leaned down to kiss her. She opened for him so he twirled his tongue with hers as the heat between them started to rise.

She slid a hand under his shirt, running her fingers through his chest hair and raking his chest with her nails. That was all it took for his dick to threaten to rip a hole right through his bottoms. Fuck, this woman got him so hot. He took his shirt off, then removed her shirt. Leaning over her, he kissed her hard, their chests pressed together. He wanted her so bad, he could taste it. He removed the rest of her clothes, and spread her gorgeous legs. Her pussy was glistening, wet with anticipation, begging for his tongue. Before he would pleasure her though, he wanted to actually hear her beg, and he knew just how to get what he wanted. He ran his fingers lightly up and down the insides of her thighs. She writhed on the bed, wanting more from him.

"Stop teasing me," she said.

"What do you want?"

"You know."

"Tell me."

She didn't respond, so he kept teasing her thighs, knowing full well how crazy he was making her. She kept shifting her body, trying desperately to get his fingers on her pussy, but he wouldn't move off her thighs. He looked her up and down, her nipples rock hard, skin flushed, chest heaving, wanting nothing more than to have him pleasure her. When she couldn't take it anymore, she cried out.

"Please, Mikael, touch my pussy," she begged.

He slid a couple fingers inside her, massaging her g-spot as he lowered his head and sucked on her clit. He loved the sweet taste of her as he sucked her harder. The intensity of her moans matched the intensity of the pleasure he was giving her. The combination of the hard pressure he put on her g-spot and her clit caused her to explode hard, drenching his fingers with her sweet honey. He removed his fingers and ran his tongue up her pussy, drinking her sweet juice, intoxicated by her taste.

"Fuck, I need to be inside you."

He slid up her soft, sexy body, and slowly thrust his dick inside her. He put his hands under her ass, and lifted her hips off the bed, allowing him even deeper penetration. He watched her face, smiling wide, her hands on her sexy breasts, rubbing them as he fucked her. Damn, she was the hottest woman he'd ever been with. He started fucking her harder, both of them screaming, a steady stream of dirty talk flying out of their mouths until their bodies had taken all they could and exploded into strong, powerful climaxes, both of them quaking from head to toe.

Mikael laid down next to her, and pulled her into his arms as she laid her head on his chest. It may have been chilly outside, but the heat inside her bedroom rivaled that of the hottest summer day. He pulled the covers up and they quickly fell asleep still holding each other. They awakened a couple hours later, happy to see the rain had been replaced by bright sunshine and warmer temperatures.

"I was thinking maybe we could pack some sandwiches and have dinner at the park," Mikael said.

"That sounds great. I just need to shower first."

"Me too, let's shower together so we can save time."

"Mmm, yes please."

They stood together in the hot steamy shower and cleaned up the aftermath of the hot sex they had earlier. When they were done, they got dressed and went to the kitchen to make sandwiches. They both decided they were in the mood for peanut butter and jelly, so they made a few sandwiches, packed up some chips, and some drinks then headed to the park. They sat at a picnic table to eat then took a walk around the park, stopping at a bench after a while to rest.

"We don't have any pictures of us yet," Mikael said.

"Only from the wedding but not since the first orgasm you gave me," she replied with a wink.

"How about we take one now?"

"Okay."

Mikael held up his phone and pulled her close then snapped a picture. She loved the way they looked together. Even more than that, she loved him. He asked her if he could share it on social media. Hannah agreed as long as he promised it was just to his friends. He posted the picture with a caption letting his friends know Hannah was his girl-friend. They sat for a little while longer enjoying the beautiful evening then headed home. They decided to do another movie night since Hannah fell asleep the last time. They made through three movies before she started getting sleepy and quickly passed out on his lap. The proximity of her head to his dick had his mind full of dirty thoughts just like last night.

"If my dick gets hard, it's going to poke her in the ear," he whispered.

"I'd rather have you stick it somewhere else," she said sleepily.

"I didn't mean to wake you."

"It's okay."

She quickly fell back asleep, as Mikael finished the movie he was watching. When it was done, he turned everything off, and gently stood up. He carried Hannah to her bed and laid her down then laid next to her, quickly joining her in a peaceful night's sleep. Sunday was a much nicer day, the sun shining bright but still with the cooler fall temperatures. Trees were just starting to turn the beautiful reds and golds of fall in Pennsylvania and the colors were breathtaking. After breakfast, they decided to take a ride in the countryside. After a couple hours of driving, they came across a scenic overlook and pulled over.

As they sat looking at the beautiful scenery, she felt his hand start running up her leg, sending the usual chills throughout her body. She covered his hand with hers and turned to look at him. He moved closer and kissed her tenderly, his tongue exploring her mouth, her panties quickly getting soaked with anticipation. She eagerly ran her tongue over his, causing his cock to spring to life. They found a more secluded spot to park, and quickly climbed in the backseat.

Hannah sat on his lap, taking the entire length of his incredible cock deep inside her, sliding up and down as he held her tight. They were fucking so hard, the entire car was shaking. She never got tired of feeling him thrusting into her, filling her pussy more than any man before him. She had her body angled perfectly, her clit rubbing his erection with every motion, her walls so stimulated that she was quickly soaring, screaming loudly as the pressure built at such a rapid pace that she almost couldn't handle it.

Her body was consumed by the most peaceful calming she'd ever felt as the rapture of their passion washed over her. She slowed her pace, increasing the pleasure even more as her pussy felt every long, slow journey up and down his massive dick until she couldn't take it anymore. Her dam broke and she soaked his cock with her powerful orgasm. Her pussy was so wet, that he slid into her even easier, quickly joining her in orgasm, his fluids mixing with hers as she collapsed onto his chest. They were completely spent, their bodies glistening with sweat.

"Fuck, that was hot," he said breathlessly.

"Especially out in the open like this," she added.

"Naughty girl," he said, as he gave her a light slap on her hot ass.

She moaned at the feeling of his hand connecting with her ass and started rocking in his lap as if she wanted more. He gave her a couple more smacks on her bottom, as she pressed her lips on his, lightly nibbling his bottom lip. He laid her back on the seat, stroking her clit with his strong fingers, as she bucked against him. His dick rock hard yet again, he fucked her even harder than she had just rode him. He pounded away at her hot pussy, feeling her hands smacking his ass like he'd just done to her, sending him quickly into orbit.

They sat in the backseat trying to catch their breath, feeling like two naughty teenagers instead of the forty-somethings they actually were, when suddenly they heard another vehicle approaching. Mikael quickly pulled a blanket over them. Hannah looked over and saw Dean's truck. They pulled in next to Mikael's car, amused looks on their faces.

"And just what were you two doing?" Dean asked.

Before Mikael could answer, Hannah said, "We just fucked each others' brains out."

Everyone laughed at Hannah's brazen answer. Hannah and Mikael got their lower halves covered back up and returned to the front seat so they could start the drive back home. After saying goodbye to Dean and Alex, Mikael backed his car up so they could turn around and get back on the road. As they were getting ready to pull out, they heard doors open and shut. Hannah looked in the mirror and saw Dean and Alex were now in the backseat of Dean's truck.

"Looks like we started something," Hannah said, laughing.

"That's my naughty, sexy woman."

Hannah watched Mikael as they drove. She still couldn't believe this man loved her. Without warning, all the joy she had felt today was replaced by fear. Something was nagging at her but she had no idea what. She suddenly had a horrible feeling in the pit of her stomach that she couldn't explain, and it scared the hell out of her. For the first time since they got together, she heard her mother's voice warn her that she was going to lose him, that he never truly loved her. She fought back tears, not wanting Mikael to know what she was feeling.

Mikael stopped at a little diner they passed on their ride so they could grab some dinner before they headed home. They took Cocoa for a quick walk then got into their jammies and snuggled under a blanket to watch some TV. They made it though about half of the first show before they were kissing, tongues dancing, hearts racing. Mikael turned the TV off and they headed to bed, spending the next couple of hours passionately making love until they were completely exhausted. They headed out to the kitchen, still naked and had a snack before heading to bed, since Hannah had to open the store in the morning.

Hannah arrived the next morning about half an hour before opening, so she had some time to check on things after the weekend. She got to her office and turned on her cell phone, having left it off all weekend so she could focus on Mikael. She went to social media and saw the picture Mikael posted it. She was surprised when she saw he made it public, after he told her it would just be for his friends to see. She noticed there was one angry face on it and when she looked to see who, she felt her stomach drop. Liza.

As Hannah's phone finished starting up, she heard a notification of a direct message and when she read it, her heart shattered. The message was from Liza, and it felt like someone was stabbing her heart repeatedly as she read her hateful words.

Don't get too settled with him. He could never truly love someone like you when he had someone like me. Get ready for heartbreak once he realizes he belongs with me back in LA, not with a nasty pig like you in Hickville, USA.

Hannah's entire body started shaking, her eyes flooding like a dam bursting after a heavy rain. Within minutes she was sobbing uncontrollably. Kurt walked into her office to sign in and rushed over to where she was sitting when he saw her. He wrapped his arms around his friend and held her close. When she had calmed a bit, he asked her what happened.

"It's over with Mikael," she sobbed.

Chapter Eleven

After Hannah showed Kurt what Mikael's ex-girlfriend wrote to her, he told her to stay in the back and he would handle the store. She promised she'd be out as soon as she composed herself. A little before noon, Mikael came in with lunch, completely unaware anything had happened. He saw Kurt at the register, but Hannah was nowhere to be found, so he approached the counter.

"Hey Kurt, Hannah around?"

"Wait here," he ordered.

Mikael was puzzled by his reaction, but figured Kurt was having a bad day. He returned from the back a few minutes later, but still no sign of his woman.

"She's busy."

"Too busy for lunch with me?"

"She said she didn't want to be disturbed."

Mikael was angry, but he didn't want to cause a scene in her store, so he thanked Kurt for checking and headed out to this car. He tried calling Hannah's cell a bunch of times, but all he got was her voicemail. He begged her to call as soon as she got his message, but by the time he got home, he still hadn't heard from her. He was about to dial her again when his phone rang. He saw Andy York's face on his screen, so he answered.

"Hey, Andy."

"Bro, what the fuck were you thinking?"

"What?"

"Why did you make that picture of you and Hannah public?"

Mikael brought up his social media and saw that Andy was right.

"Fuck. I forgot to change the setting."

He went into a panic when he saw that Liza had reacted with an angry face. Kurt's attitude and Hannah's refusal to see him was starting to make more sense. He didn't see any comments on the post, but he knew that wasn't the only way Liza could get to her. He frantically dialed Hannah's cell over and over, but still no answer, so he got in his car and raced back to the pet shop.

He parked next to Hannah's and waited until she closed up and came outside. He saw her and Kurt walk out together, along with Cocoa. He got out of his car and approached them. Kurt stopped him and told him Hannah didn't want to see him. He ignored Kurt and asked Hannah what was going on.

"Leave me alone," she said quietly.

"What's wrong?"

"Just go home."

"Talk to me, baby. Please," he begged.

"She asked you to leave her alone. Respect her wishes and go," Kurt told him.

"I'm not leaving until you tell me what she said."

"Like you fucking care. Was this just a cruel joke between you and Liza?"

"You can't be serious."

"I always knew my mom was right about me. No one would want a woman like me."

"You know that's not true. I think I've proven to you how I feel."

"Yeah right. Well, you can call your girlfriend and let her know she won."

"Please, I love you. Come home with me so we can talk."

"No. Mikael. Go the hell back to LA where you belong."

She put Cocoa in her backseat then got in her car and drove off. Mikael just stood there dumbfounded. He turned to Kurt, feeling more desperate then he ever had before. He loved that woman and he couldn't bear the thought of even one night without her warm body next to him in bed.

"Did she tell you anything?"

"Yeah, asshole she did. Liza told her that you could never really love her and told her she was a nasty pig. She was devastated."

Before Mikael had a chance to respond, Kurt got in his car, slammed the door and raced out of the parking lot. Mikael got in his car and just sat there, completely in shock. How could the same woman he spent hours making love to the night before suddenly refuse to even talk to him. He started his car and headed out of the parking lot. A few minutes later, he pulled into Dean's driveway, got out and rang their doorbell. Alex came to the door, her smile quickly disappearing when she saw his face. She walked him into the living room where Dean was sitting on the couch.

"Dude, you look like hell."

Barely audible, he said, "Thanks a lot."

"Sorry, man. What's going on?"

"Hannah won't see me or talk to me."

Alex put her hand on his arm. "What happened?"

Mikael filled them in on his fuck up with posting the picture and Liza's comments to Hannah.

"What can I do?" Alex asked.

"I hate to put you in this position, but I need someone to help me convince her my feelings are real."

"I volunteered and if you are okay with waiting until tomorrow, I want to give her a night to calm down first."

"Okay. I can't tell you how much I appreciate this."

"You two belong together, so I'm happy to help."

"Thank you both."

Mikael wanted nothing more than to drive to Hannah's house but she made it clear that she needed space so he headed home. He wandered around his house for a while, completely restless. He was aching without his beautiful woman in his arms and he hated that feeling. He hadn't felt that way since he was with Liza. He logged onto his social media account and saw that he had a message from Liza asking if he was ready to come home yet. Bitch. He just deleted it, not wanting to ever deal with her again. After a couple of hours of staring at the TV, he finally went to bed. Sleep eluded him without her there. He would do anything it took to get her back.

Hannah didn't fare much better, her night restless at best. She was finally able to get some sleep but still woke up feeling pretty crappy. Her only solace was having Cocoa laying next to her, pressed against Hannah, as if knowing she needed comforting. She got up the next morning and somehow was able to get ready for work. She put herself on auto-pilot to get through the day without alienating any customers. Around lunchtime, she started looking for Mikael out of habit, but he didn't come, which did nothing to help her mood. She went back to her office to eat and take a little break.

A few minutes after she went in, Kurt knocked on the door and let her know Alex was there, so Hannah told him to send her back. Alex came in and give her friend a big hug then sat down. Hannah could tell by the look on her face that she knew something happened with Mikael. Dean was his only friend in town besides Hannah, so she wasn't surprise to hear Alex tell her he stopped by last night.

"I'm so sorry at what Liza said, but you do know she's wrong, don't you?"

"Yeah right, Mikael thinks I'm a joke."

"Stop it, he does not."

"My mom was right."

"Your mom? I don't understand."

Hannah filled Alex in on what her mom had put her through and how she was able to confront her when she showed up at the store.

"Her voice finally disappeared out of my head after Mikael and I started having sex. Then I get this," she said, handing Alex her phone.

Alex read the full message from Liza and said, "Stupid bitch. She doesn't know shit about you or how Mikael feels about you."

"I'm sure all Mikael feels is disgust."

"I see the way he looks at you. Girl, he loves you."

"Sure he does. He goes from a stunning model like Liza to a frumpy farm girl?"

"You are about as far from frumpy as I can think of. I remember that dress you wore to my wedding. Mikael was practically drooling. I thought he was going to need a bib."

That got a small laugh out of Hannah, though it didn't last. Sadness quickly returned as she sat and thought about him. Another round of tears spilled over as Hannah walked over and sat down on the couch in her office. Alex sat next to her, hugging her friend.

"I know you probably don' want to hear this, but maybe you should talk to him. He loves you."

"I can't. All I see when I close my eyes is the two of them laughing at the nasty pig."

"You are not a nasty pig. You are, however, a kind, beautiful, intelligent woman and that man loves you."

"I appreciate the sentiment, but I just can't get past this."

"I'm not going to push you, but please, take some time to think about it before you make any rash decisions."

"I'll think about it. Best I can give you right now."

"Just don't wait too long and lose your shot. I almost did with Dean, but look at us now."

Hannah smiled, remembering how happy Alex looked on her wedding day. She hadn't lost one bit of that glow. She and Dean were lucky to have each other. If only she could have had that with Mikael, but she knew in her heart he would never truly be satisfied with anyone other than those skinny little LA women, not someone who looked like her. He sure did a good job pretending, but that was probably just to get laid, she thought to herself.

After Alex left, Hannah went back out front. Business was booming today, helping her get through the rest of the day without thinking about Mikael. No such luck that would continue when she got home. Her mother's voice was especially prominent now, full of nasty laughing and "I told you so." By the time she was done, Hannah felt worse about herself then she ever had. She knew there was no way she could ever see Mikael again. It would hurt too much, knowing that she could never be with him. She would never be enough for him and she had to accept that and find a way to move on.

When Alex got home, she filled Dean in on her talk with Hannah. He was pissed that bitch was still messing up Mikael's life. They called

Mikael and invited him over for dinner so they could fill him in. He was so angry at what Liza did, he barely even touched his dinner. His insides ached with the pain of not having his woman. More than that, though, he ached knowing how much what Liza said hurt Hannah. He had finally been able to get her to believe what he knew, that she was beautiful and now the she-devil had completely undone it.

"What am I going to do?"

"You need to tell her again how you feel," Dean responded.

"How the fuck do I do that when she won't even talk to me. Sorry, I know you're just trying to help."

"It's okay. I know how I'd feel if it were Alex not wanting to talk to me."

"Karaoke," Alex said.

She filled Dean and Mikael in on a plan she had come up with. Hannah could never say no to Karaoke, so Alex said she would invite to her for a girls night. She described the rest of the plan in detail, and Mikael finally felt a glimmer of hope that he would get his woman back in his life, in his bed, in his arms. Alex grabbed her phone and dialed Hannah, putting the phone on speaker.

"Hello."

"Hey, it's Alex. How would you like a girls night?"

"I'm not really up for going out."

"Come on you can't make me do Karaoke alone."

I really don't want to."

"Please! For me!"

Having no fight left in her, she said, "Fine."

"I'll be over in about an hour, if that gives you enough time."

"I'll be ready."

After they disconnected, Hannah grabbed a shower and got ready to go. The plan was for Mikael and Dean to head to the club now, and wait backstage. When the Karaoke starts, the plan is for Mikael to come out and sing a love song to Hannah, hoping that will at least get her to talk to him. He thanked Alex over and over before they headed out. Alex drove over and picked up Hannah then they also headed to the club. She felt a little bit guilty for tricking Hannah, but she knew that her and Mikael belonged together.

When they arrived, Alex sent a text to Dean, letting him know they were there. Doug came up on stage and announced the start of Karaoke and that the first performer was waiting backstage. A romantic song start playing. After a minute, Mikael walked out and Hannah instantly burst into tears.

"What the fuck," she screamed at Alex.

"You belong with him and you know it."

"Fuck you." Hannah yelled and ran out.

Great, she thought, now I'm stuck her with no ride. She was about to call a cab when she felt a hand on her shoulder. She turned and saw Kurt standing there. He had seen her run out and followed her in case she needed a friend. He offered to drive her home, which she gladly accepted. She couldn't believe her friend would do this to her. When they got to her driveway, Hannah thanked Kurt then got out of the car and walked around to the driver's side.

"Can you handle the store by yourself for a couple days?"

"Of course."

"Thanks. I need to get away from here for a bit. I'm going to take Cocoa and go camping."

"Have a peaceful time. I'm always here if you need an ear. And hey, don't be too hard on Alex. I'm sure she meant well."

Hannah forced a smile, but she was still pissed as hell they did that to her. She waved as Kurt pulled out then headed inside. She let Cocoa out then locked up and went straight to bed, again crying herself to sleep, missing Mikael's warm body next to hers. Of course, she had a dirty dream about him, making her miss him even more.

Chapter Twelve

Hannah got up early the next morning and packed up what she needed for her camping getaway. She loved having a cabin she could go to for relaxing and decompressing, which was exactly what she needed right now. She had always been more of a tomboy and enjoyed things like camping and fishing. Once she had her car loaded, she and Cocoa headed out. Her cabin was about three hours away, and it was a beautiful country drive with very little traffic.

Once she arrived and unloaded her car, she sat down on the couch trying to free her mind of Mikael. Easier said than done, so she decided to grab her fishing gear and walk down to the pond. It was a perfect fall day, sunny and blue skies cool enough that she wasn't sweating but warm enough that jeans and a t-shirt were enough. She fished for several hours, finally starting to relax. As it was approaching dinnertime, and because it was starting to get dark earlier, she decided to head back.

After getting Cocoa her dinner, she made her favorite comfort meal, a grilled cheese sandwich and a bowl of tomato soup. She sat down at the dinette table in the kitchen, wishing Mikael was sitting across from her. As hard as she tried, she just couldn't get him out of her head. After she ate, she curled up on the couch with the latest steamy romance novel she was reading, and of course imagined it was she and Mikael in all the dirty scenes. Tired from the drive and everything she'd been through the last couple of days, she locked up and headed to bed.

She woke up the next morning feeling fairly well-rested and decided to go for a hike around the lake. She loved taking Cocoa for long walks, which of course, Cocoa was always overjoyed to do. Sometimes she wished she could switch places with her furry friend. She always thought it would be so much better to be a dog, taking delight in something as simple as a new scent. After several hours of walking, Hannah stopped to have a quick bite to eat and give Cocoa some water and a couple treats.

When they were done, they started the rest of their walk, planning to do a complete circle and end up back at the cabin. Cocoa suddenly caught sight of a rabbit and took off, pulling Hannah to the ground. When she tried to get up, she realized she had twisted her ankle and couldn't put any pressure on it. Shit, she thought, there's only one person who knows where my cabin is. Even though she was still mad at Alex, she had no choice but to call her. Luckily, Alex picked up right away.

"Hey Hannah."

"Hi. Sorry to bother you, but I'm stuck and I need your help."

"Where are you?"

"The cabin. I needed some time away, especially after what happened at Karaoke."

"Car trouble?"

"No, Cocoa ran after a rabbit and pulled me down, and I injured my ankle."

"I'm leaving now. Be there as fast as I can."

"Thank you."

Alex didn't tell Hannah that Mikael was there, as she didn't want to upset her. She asked Dean if he would come with her so one of them could drive Hannah's car back in case she couldn't. Dean was about to grab his keys and a jacket when Mikael stopped him.

"Please let me drive. If she wants me to leave, I'll go and you can drive her car back."

Alex looked at Dean who nodded yes.

"Okay, let's go," she said. "It's a three hour drive so I don't want Hannah sitting outside when it gets dark."

"Dean, would you do me a favor?" Mikael asked.

"Anything."

"Could you pick up Leo and bring his litter box and food over so he's not alone?"

"I have a study group, so I'll pick him up on my way home."

"Thanks, man."

They got into Mikael's car and headed out.

"I just need to stop home and grab something quick," he announced.

"Okay."

Alex waited in the car until Mikael came back out. Once he was done, they started their journey to rescue his beautiful woman. Mikael exceeded the speed limit the entire way there and they made it to the gas station near the cabin in about two hours. He pulled in, handed Alex his credit card and asked her to fill the tank.

"What are you doing?" she asked.

"I need to go change."

Alex gave him a puzzled look but didn't ask any questions. She finished pumping the gas and got back in the car. She almost died laughing when she saw him. Mikael was now dressed in a superhero costume, so tight that you could see every muscle, every everything, especially what he was packing in his pants. No wonder Hannah looked so happy once they got together.

"What?" was all she could manage to say.

"I'm going to rescue my damsel in distress."

"I would normally make fun of you and call you a nerd for a costume like this, but one thing I know about my friend is her love of all things superhero. If you have any chance of winning her back, this is the way to do it."

He smiled as they finished the last half-hour of their drive. When they pulled up in front of the cabin, Alex called Hannah to get as close to her exact location as she could. She let Alex know she was doing a lap around the lake and which direction to head so her walk would be shorter. Alex and Mikael started out and knew they were close when they heard Cocoa barking.

Hannah looked up and saw two figures approaching, at first thinking it was Dean with her. When they got closer, she thought she was hallucinating when she saw a superhero walking next to Alex. Mikael ran ahead and raced over to where Hannah had been sitting. She tried her damnedest not to laugh, but she couldn't help it.

"What on earth?" she asked in between giggles.

"I'm here to rescue you, my damsel."

She felt all the anger and devastation melt away as her hero carried her back to the cabin. She also couldn't be mad at Alex anymore. When they got inside, Mikael laid her down on the couch, and placed a pillow under her foot. She looked at them both, her heart filled with so much love that they would come help her like this after the way she'd acted the past couple of days.

"I'm so sorry for yelling at you," she said to Alex. "I know you were only trying to help."

"Thank you, but I'm also sorry for tricking you."

"All is forgiven."

"For me too. Do you think you'll be okay to drive tomorrow?"

"I'm not sure."

"Okay, then to be safe, one of us is going to drive your car home tonight and the other will stay with you. Your choice."

"No offense, Alex, but I really need to talk to Mikael."

"That is the only answer I would have accepted. I'm going to head out so most of my drive is still in the light. Get some rest."

"Thanks again."

Alex grabbed Hannah's keys and headed home, leaving her alone with Mikael. She couldn't help but smile at him sitting there dressed like a superhero. Who was she kidding, he was a superhero and she loved him, but she did need to explain her behavior the last several days. Before she did, she wanted to ice her ankle, so she started to get up.

"What are you doing?"

"I need to get some ice for my ankle."

"Sit tight, I'll get it."

Speaking of tight, holy shit. That costume left nothing to the imagination. She kept her eyes on his sexy ass the whole time he was putting an ice pack together. At least she was until he turned around then, of course, her eyes immediately went to the eggplant he was smuggling. Seeing where her eyes were focused, he cleared his throat, feigning annoyance.

"My eyes are up here, not down there," he said, pointing at his crotch.

She laughed as he handed her the ice bag. She needed to get serious for a few minutes, so she took a deep breath before she started talking.

"I'm sorry for how I've been acting," she whispered.

"No, I'm sorry for what Liza said. I called her up and tore her a new asshole."

"I don't know why I let it get to me so much."

"After what you told me about your mom, I understand."

"I'm also sorry about Karaoke. The song was beautiful, but I just wasn't ready."

"I shouldn't have pushed, but I missed you so much. I couldn't stand the pain of not having you."

"I felt the same way. I love you."

"I love you. Does this mean we're back together?"

"How could I say no to anyone who does this for me," she said, pointing at his costume. "You're by far the sexiest superhero EVER! Is that costume yours or did you rent it?"

"It's mine, why?"

"Good, we may need that again."

She wouldn't elaborate, but he hoped like hell she had something naughty in mind. When the ice pack started to melt, he took it and put it in the freezer. He saw her start yawning and asked her if she was ready to head to bed.

"I think so, tough day today."

"I'll help you get settled then I'll make up the couch for myself."

"Like hell you will. I need to be in your arms tonight. I need to hold off on anything else because of my ankle, but I don't want to sleep alone ever again."

"You got it baby."

He picked her up off the couch and carried her into the bathroom and waited until she was done then carried her to bed and gently laid her down. He started to take off his costume to join her.

"Leave it on."

"What?"

"I've always wanted to sleep with a superhero."

He smiled and joined her in bed. He laid behind her and wrapped her arms around her. She nestled herself into his arms and quickly drifted off to sleep. He woke up the next morning, his beautiful woman still wrapped in his arms. He lightly kissed the top of her head and she stirred, slowly waking up. After turning to face him, she leaned in and eagerly pressed her lips to his.

"Know what else I've always want to do?" she asked.

"What?"

"Fuck a superhero."

She unzipped his costume and ran her tongue all over his bare chest. As she moved lower to open more of the costume, she looked up and smiled when she saw his dick was hard. Once he was naked, she wrapped her mouth around his dick, sucking him hard and fast. Unable to control himself, he quickly filled her mouth with his salty goodness, watching as she swallowed him down. He laid her on her back and quickly removed her clothes. He couldn't take his eyes off this gorgeous woman, lying there completely naked, eager to feel his touch.

Starting at her neck, he ran his tongue straight down the center of her body until he reached her sweet pussy. He covered her with his mouth, his tongue working her clit hard. She moaned and writhed on the bed, the intensity of the pleasure causing her to quickly soar. He would never tire of her taste, of feeling her body explode when he brought her to the point of no return, hearing her scream his name.

His cock throbbed with desire, wanting nothing more than to be wrapped in the warmth of her. He slid up her beautiful body, and plunged inside her as deep as he could. Fuck, it felt so good inside her. He slowly and sensually slid his dick in and out of her pussy, still slick from her orgasm. He wrapped his arms around her, holding on tight, kissing her passionately as they continued their lovemaking. When they were done, he moved next to her and pulled her into his arms, loving the feeling of being with her.

They got up and showered, then headed to the kitchen to have some breakfast. They decided to spend another night at the cabin and head home the following day. Mikael wanted to spend the day at the lake. He noticed a small rowboat tied to the dock.

"Yours?"

"Yes it is."

"Let's go."

Cocoa jumped in the boat, as she loved going for rides then Mikael helped Hannah in. He pushed the boat into the water then got in himself and rowed the around the lake. The view was breathtaking, especially the view sitting across from him. He loved what fall on the East Coast looked like, the trees turning the most beautiful colors. He knew he was exactly where he belonged, and more importantly he knew he was with the person with whom he belonged. He rowed them to the center of the lake, stopping there to kiss her.

He rowed over to the side of the lake furthest from the cabin onto the shore and got out of the boat. He held it steady for Hannah who then helped Cocoa out. Hannah had a long rope that she secured around a tree, clipping the other end to Cocoa's collar, allowing her to have plenty of room to run, but not having to worry about her taking off or getting lost. Mikael laid down in the grass, Hannah joining him. They embraced, facing each other, as Mikael crushed his lips to hers. He felt her tongue tracing his bottom lip, driving him wild. He felt his dick stirring.

"Baby, I wanna make love right here by the lake," he whispered softly.

"Mmm, yes please. I've never done it outside before, but always wanted to."

There was something so primal about being naked with him out here in the open. She pushed him on his back and mounted him, sliding her sweet body down on his, taking his dick deep inside her. She positioned herself so that her clit rubbed his dick as she rode him. She matched his pace from earlier, moving up and down so slowly, he thought he was going to lose his mind. Nothing had ever felt as good as being inside her, watching her let loose and truly enjoy herself. Nothing was hotter than a woman who wasn't afraid to explore her sexuality. He felt the pressure building as he matched her with his own powerful thrusts until they came together, perfectly in sync.

He held her tight as she collapsed down on to his chest, then moved next to him. They held each other, the grass tickling their naked bodies. The warm fall sun shone down on them as Mikael moved on top of her. They made love several more times in the warm grass then got dressed and headed back to the cabin to have an early dinner. After they finished eating, they took Cocoa for a walk, heading back when the sun started its descent. They air was quickly turning chilly as the sun disappeared over the horizon, so they went inside. Both exhausted from their fun-filled day, they went to bed and quickly fell asleep holding each other.

Chapter Thirteen

They woke up early the next morning and packed up to head home. Hannah wanted to try to give Kurt a break since he had been running the shop by himself. She also needed to get over to Alex's to get her car. They stopped and grabbed breakfast to go since Cocoa was with them and ate in the parking lot before they got back on the road. Hannah felt a million times better than when she had come up to cabin, so grateful to have her sexy man back in her life, and of course, in her bed.

She heard a text come in on her phone and saw it was from Alex letting her know she had left her car at her house, so she didn't have to pick it up. When they got back, Mikael helped Hannah carry all her stuff in then headed home to shower. Hannah did the same then headed to the store. Kurt let her know everything had been fine while she was away. She gave him the rest of the week off with pay to thank him for covering.

After he showered, Mikael drove down to the store. Since she was alone, she temporarily closed for lunch. They decided to grab lunch at the new cafe across the street. 'The Garden of Eden' was a combination tea and coffee bar and a bookstore, also serving salads and cold sandwiches. They had only been open about a week, so there weren't many customers yet. The owner, Eden Mitchell, greeted them at the door and took them to a table. She returned a minute later with two menus.

"I'm Hannah. I own the pet shop across the street."

"Nice to meet you."

"Same. Since you're so new, I would love to help drive some customers to your cafe. Do you have any fliers or anything? I could put them on the counter, plus give them out to shoppers."

"You'd be willing to do that? I couldn't pay you."

"No need to worry about that. I was a brand new business once and I remember what it was like."

"Thank you so much. Whatever you order is on the house today."

"That's kind, but I'd like to pay to help you out."

"Thank you. I'll give you both a couple minutes with the menu."

Mikael and Hannah both decided on the chicken Caesar salad and a cup of herbal tea. Eden gave the order to her cook then brought them hot water and a few tea bags. A little while later, their salads came out. Everything was delicious. When they were done, Eden brought over their check, which Mikael quickly grabbed. He added an extra 50% to help Eden out. She tried to refuse, but Mikael wouldn't take no for an answer.

"If you ever need any advice or help, give me a shout," Hannah said, as she handed Eden a piece of paper with her cell phone number on it.

"Thank you so much. I have to print some fliers then I'll drop some off."

"Awesome. Best of luck with everything. The place looks beautiful."

They headed back to the pet shop to open up. The afternoon was pretty busy, so Mikael stayed and helped out so Hannah wouldn't be by herself. Once they hit closing time, he helped her get things ready for the morning then walked her to her car.

"You wanna spend the night?" he asked.

"I'd love to, under one condition."

"Name it."

"I could use a soak in your tub."

"You got it! I'll follow you home so you can drop your car off then we'll head to my house. You're in for a night of well-deserved pampering."

"Sounds perfectly divine. Just one small change. Can you take Cocoa to you house and I'll meet you there?"

"Why?"

Hannah flashed a wicked smile that made his heart beat faster but she wouldn't say a word. He dropped her off, and raced home, eagerly anticipating what she had in store for him. She hadn't told him about the outfit she ordered when they first started talking about role play. She changed then packed herself an overnight bag and headed to his house. She had a feeling he was going to like what he saw.

Mikael was sitting in his living room when he heard a loud knock on his door. He opened the door and his jaw dropped.

"I'm Officer Davidson. I was told you've been a very naughty boy."

He was unable to even speak. The sexiest damn cop he'd ever seen was standing outside his front door, twirling a pair of furry handcuffs. She had on a tight blouse with a couple buttons open, showing quite a bit of cleavage. She was also wearing a very short leather skirt and thigh high boots. She turned her back to him and bent over, showing him that she had no panties on. He was finding it almost impossible to even catch his breath.

"Do you admit to the charges?"

He nodded.

"I can't hear you," she said sternly.

"Yeah."

"Then you're under arrest. Turnaround and put your hands behind your back." She snapped the cuffs on his wrists and commanded, "Bedroom. NOW!"

He walked into the bedroom with her close behind him. When he got inside, she gave him a hard slap on his ass, sending him into overdrive, and he could feel his dick starting to stir.

"Walk over to the bed and bend over so I can give you your punishment!"

He bent over and put his head on the bed. Officer Hannah stood behind him and gave him a couple more hard smacks on his ass, as he growled with pleasure. She moved him where she wanted him to stand, removed the cuffs then walked over to the chair and sat down. She spread her legs wide, giving him a full view of her naked pussy.

"Strip for me. Slowly."

He removed his sneakers and socks first then slowly pulled his t-shirt over his head. He watched as she licked her lips while she ran her hand down her body. He took his jeans off, standing there in just his under-wear, dick hard as a rock. Hannah looked down at his bulge, and started stroking her pussy. He thought he was going to pass out cold watching her touch herself.

"You're not done. Get that underwear off!"

He did as she commanded, his dick springing up once it was released from its cage. Still pleasuring herself, she commanded him to lay on the bed. She walked over, furry cuffs in hand. She grabbed his wrists one at a time and cuffed him to the headboard. He had never been as turned on in his entire life as he was now.

She climbed onto the bed, straddling him. The feeling of her leather boots against his skin was driving him wild. He wanted nothing more than to rip her clothes off, but he couldn't move. He watched as she slowly unbuttoned her shirt, tossing it to the floor, followed by her bra. Damn, he never got tired of seeing her naked tits. She crawled up his body until her pussy was just barely touching his cock. She lowered her body down on his throbbing cock, taking every last inch of him inside of her.

Her leather skirt and boots were tickling his legs as she slid her hot pussy up and down his shaft, her tits bouncing wildly. She unbuttoned the skirt and tossed it the floor, giving him full view of her curvy body. Fuck, he loved seeing all that naked skin. She rode him hard and fast, screaming loudly, as his massive dick was rubbing her clit and her g-spot.

"I want you to taste me," she said as she slid off his dick.

She moved next to him, angling her body so her pussy was next to his head. He plunged his tongue into her, licking up every drop of her delicious honey. He moved his tongue to her swollen clit, licking hard as she bucked her hips, moaning loudly.

"Fuck, that's so damn good."

Without warning she pulled away. She crawled down the bed, giving him full view of her hot naked ass. She climbed back onto his dick, again riding him hard, as he matched her rhythm with powerful thrusts. Suddenly, he felt her entire body start quaking as she drenched his cock, experiencing orgasms from her g-spot and clit simultaneously. The entire scene was so hot that he lost all control and filled her pussy with his salty cream.

"Holy, shit, woman. And you say I'm naughty."

"Who me? I'm a perfect angel," she laughed.

"My ass."

"Your ass is pretty fuckin' sexy."

"Just like that outfit. Now, though, it's my turn since you've been quite naughty yourself."

"Does that mean it's my turn to get punished?"

"Your damn right, woman. Get me out of these cuffs then bend that hot ass over the bed!"

She bent over, but instead of getting spanked, he stood behind her and entered her pussy from behind. He pounded her hard and fast, as she moaned loudly. It felt incredible when he fucked her like this. He gave her a couple of light smacks on her ass as he kept pounding her red hot pussy.

"Oh fuck, so good."

With the rapid thrusts he was giving her, they both quickly exploded in intense orgasms.

"Lay on the bed, baby."

She started to remove her boots.

"Stop! Leave those sexy boots on."

She laid down on the bed and Mikael joined her, spreading her legs wide. He lowered his mouth onto her mound and started sucking hard. She writhed on the bed as he worked his magic on her. He slid up her body and slid inside her, slower and more passionately then before, truly making love to her this time. She wrapped her arms around him as he pulled her close, kissing her softly as their bodies moved together.

"I love you," he whispered.

"I love you so much."

They rocked each other's bodies until again they rode that ultimate wave of pleasure together. Mikael moved next to her and held her close, kissing her mouth, loving the taste of both of them on her tongue.

"Damn, woman, so hot. Now, how about we go take that soak?"

"Mmm, yes please, baby."

"Wait here."

He went into the bathroom to start the tub then disappeared down-stairs. He returned a few minutes later with wine, a couple of glasses, and a cheese and cracker platter. He put everything down near the tub, and walked into the bedroom. He took her hands and sat her up. Kneeling down, he removed her boots one at a time, running his hands down her legs, setting her entire body on fire. He helped her up and they walked into the bathroom. She saw that he had filled the tub with bubbles.

He helped her into the tub, then climbed in next to her. She sighed contentedly, feeling completely relaxed as the jets massaged her body. Mikael poured two glasses of wine and handed one to her.

"To us, my love," he said.

"Cheers to you, sexy."

They ate some of the cheese and crackers and finished their wine. After they were done, they both leaned back, in heaven at the feeling of being in the warm water, naked skin touching each other, completely in love with each other. They both quickly dozed off, much needed after their incredible romp in his bed. They awakened about an hour later, both of them starving. They got into the shower to rinse the bubbles off then got dressed and headed out to grab some pizza.

When they got home from dinner, they loaded Cocoa up in the car and drove to the dog park. They saw Dean and Chris's cars when they pulled into the parking lot. Chris's girls were playing with Daisy and Holly. When they got inside the fence, they took Cocoa's leash off and she ran over to play with the others. Mikael went over and sat with Dean and Chris, while Alex waved Hannah over to join her and Tracey.

Both groups sat and talked until the girls came over and told Tracey the dogs were all laying down. Hannah looked over and saw three very tired dogs lying in the grass together. They went over and leashed all the dogs then joined the men. With the shit-eatin' grins they were all sport-ing, she had a feeling she knew what they had been talking about. Hannah teased him on the ride home, but Mikael wouldn't break the "bro code" and refused to spill any details.

When they got home, Hannah kept pestering him about what the guys were talking about He picked her up, put her over his shoulder and carried her to the bedroom. Every time she asked what they were talking about, she got a swat on her ass. She was so turned on by the time they reached the bedroom, her panties were soaked. Mikael put her down, laid on top of her and kissed her hard, lightly biting her bottom lip as she moaned into his mouth.

She wanted him so bad that she couldn't keep her hands to herself. She opened his jeans, and slid her hand inside his underwear, stroking his cock until he was rock hard. She ached to feel him deep inside her and starting writhing on the bed. He quickly undressed her then himself. He climbed back on top of her, spread her legs wide, and slid the entire length of his dick inside her, stroking her g-spot hard as every powerful thrust rubbed hard against her clit. Within moments, her body was quaking as she rode wave after wave of pleasure. Watching her explode sent him over the edge and he filled her with a huge load of his hot cum. Spent from their hot passionate fuck, they quickly fell asleep holding each other.

Chapter Fourteen

"Boy, do I have a surprise for you," Mikael said, a huge smile on his gorgeous face.

"Tell me, tell me, tell me," Hannah exclaimed.

"You favorite band's doing a show at the Hard Rock in Atlantic City."

He turned his laptop around and she squealed with delight, seeing those four sexy men in full costumes and makeup. Even though the band had seen several personnel changes, the two main members remained steady. She'd loved this band since she was a little girl, and seen them live a few times, never disappointed with the show they put on.

"I was able to call in a favor. We have front row tickets and VIP passes to meet them," Mikael told her.

"OH MY GOD," she screamed, jumping up and down, tears of joy streaming down her face.

"Do you think Kurt could cover for a couple days? I booked us a suite for three nights."

"I might actually close instead."

"Cool. We leave Thursday and come home Sunday. And you better be ready for some dirty fun."

She was completely without words, she was so excited. She hugged him tight, still bouncing with excitement. He kissed her hard, awakening that familiar heat in her body. Nothing felt better than being in his hot, sexy arms. Well, almost nothing. When they were naked and fucking, there was nothing on earth quite like that.

Hannah headed into work and let Kurt know she would be closing, and that he would be paid for the time he would have worked. He thanked her, grateful for the time off. She was sitting in her office going over inventory when panic set in, thinking about what he might have planned for her. She grabbed her cell.

"Hello."

"Alex, I need your help!"

"What's up?"

"Mikael's taking me to Atlantic City for a few days. I need a shopping partner. Also, would you guys mind taking care of Cocoa and Leo?"

"I'm free tonight. Dean has a class. I'll meet you at the shop after you close. And of course, we'd be glad to pet-sit."

"Thank you so much."

"You're welcome."

After they disconnected, Hannah finished up her work then headed out front. She was having a hard time focusing on anything other than Atlantic City. She was still in disbelief that she would be meeting her all-time favorite band. Mikael came into the shop around noon with lunch. He loved seeing that her excitement hadn't dropped even a little. The concert was going to be amazing, but even more than that, he kept thinking about what he wanted to do to her while they were in their suite. He ended up staying for the rest of the day, a welcome help as the shop got busy in the afternoon. Once the last customer was taken care of, Hannah told Kurt to head home and enjoy his evening.

She started walking around the store, checking to see if any shelves needed straightening. Mikael grabbed the vacuum and started helping her clean up. Once they finished out front, Hannah walked back to her office to count the tills and put get her deposit ready for the bank. After she had locked the money in her safe, she sat down on her desk. She looked over at Mikael and saw a naughty smile creep across his face.

Without a word, he got up and walked over to her, placing himself between her legs. He wrapped his arms around her and kissed her, his tongue eagerly exploring her mouth. He lifted her shirt over her head and again pressed his lips to hers. She felt him undo and remove her bra, his hands massaging her breasts. She unbuttoned and removed his shirt, exposing his sexy, muscular chest. She loved the warmth of his skin against hers, as her pussy throbbed with desire, aching to be filled by his massive cock.

"Get naked and get that hot ass back on the desk," he commanded.

"No!"

"Excuse me."

"This is my store, so that means I'm in charge. Undress me, now."

She stood so he could remove her clothes. When she was naked, she sat back on the desk and spread her legs wide.

"On your knees now. I want you to eat my pussy until I explode."

Mikael knelt in front of her, his hands on her thighs. He ran his tongue up and down her pussy, making her moan. He flicked his tongue over her clit.

"Suck my clit hard, baby."

He wrapped his lips around her swollen clit, sucking her hard. She bucked her hips and threw her head back, screaming in pleasure. Her entire body shook as she came hard.

"Now, get those pants off and get on the couch."

Mikael removed his pants and underwear, freeing his rock hard cock. Once he sat, Hannah stood in front of him.

"Tell me what you want."

"I want your pussy on my cock."

"I wanna hear you beg."

"Baby, please sit on my cock. I need to feel your hot, wet pussy sliding up and down me. My dick is throbbing with desire for you."

She lowered herself into his lap, holding onto to his sexy arms for support. She moved her hips up and down, her breasts bouncing in his face. He took turns sucking each breast, his tongue flicking her nipples. They were both moaning loud as they fucked like animals, and they didn't hear the door to the shop open.

As she exploded hard, drenching his dick as she rode wave after wave of pleasure, she screamed loudly. Her orgasm was so sexy, he quickly came inside her.

"Oh fuck, Mikael, you make my pussy feel so damn incredible."

She collapsed against her hot bass god, both of them breathing hard as he embraced his beautiful woman, his dick still inside her. She grabbed the tissue box next to the couch so they could clean up a bit, then got dressed. They walked out and came face to face with Alex, who was standing there with an amused look on her face.

"Hi Alex," Hannah said sheepishly.

"Hi. Working a little late?"

"Um, something like that."

"That's what I figured. Ready to go?"

Hannah turned to look at Mikael, "We're going shopping for the trip."

Mikael, who refused to take his eyes off the floor, said, "Okay. See you when you're done."

"Okay," Hannah replied.

Mikael walked them out, still unable to look at Alex, waving to Hannah as they got in Hannah's car and headed toward the mall. He took that chance to go do some shopping of his own. He had a really fun weekend planned for his sexy woman. Once he was done, he headed home to wait for her. Dean was sitting on his porch when he pulled in, as his class had ended. By the look on his face, Mikael knew Alex had told him what she heard. As Mikael walked up to the porch, Dean stood and bowed to him.

"Funny, asshole."

"Alex told me she got quite an earful. And here I thought Hannah was a good girl," Dean quipped.

"That she most definitely is not."

"We are definitely two lucky fuckers. Alex and Hannah are amazing."

"Yes they are."

While their men sat at Mikael's house drinking beers and shooting the shit, Hannah and Alex were walking around the mall.

"I'm a little embarrassed about what I'm about to ask," Hannah said quietly.

"Don't be, it's just me."

"I want some sexy stuff to wear, like some bedroom stuff. I usually only do that kind of shopping on line."

"Let's go."

They headed down to the store that specialized in exactly what Hannah was looking for. They spent about an hour in there and Hannah was happy with what she found.

"Girl, that man is going to lose his shit when he sees you," Alex told her.

"Exactly what I was going for."

"I get the feeling there's a lot I never knew about you."

"Maybe," Hannah said, grinning.

"Damn, girl."

Hannah had a huge smile on her face as she pictured what Mikael might do to her when he saw her in some of those outfits they bought. After they grabbed her a couple of things to wear to the concert and just around the casino, they headed home. They pulled in and saw their men on the porch. Hannah honked her horn repeatedly while Alex whistled at them. After Dean and Alex left, Hannah and Mikael went inside to have a light dinner and a relaxing night in front of the TV. They made it though a half of a show before they were naked and fucking on his couch.

The next couple days crawled by. Hannah couldn't wait until their trip, especially getting to meet her favorite band. By Wednesday afternoon, she was bouncing off the walls and driving Kurt crazy. Mikael stopped by at lunchtime with some food. Kurt filled him on how crazy his woman was, laughing at her practically floating around the store. After they all finished eating, Hannah gave Kurt the rest of the day off, which he gladly accepted. The afternoon was slow, but at least having Mikael there, she wasn't bored.

When they were done, they walked back to her office for her nightly routine of counting up the money and getting the deposit ready. Mikael stood behind her the whole time she was working. Feeling his warm breath on her neck was driving her wild and she felt herself getting wet with desire. After she had the money in the safe, she stood in front of him, hands on her hips, with a stern look on her face. Not saying a word, she did a slow striptease for him, his dick straining against his jeans as he watched more and more of her beautiful naked skin appear. She walked over to the couch and knelt, holding the back for support.

"Get over here and get that dick inside me."

Mikael quickly took his clothes off and stood behind her, sliding every inch of his cock deep inside her. He took one hand and grabbed her breast, stroking her clit with the other as he pounded her hard. They were both groaning loudly as the pressure built in their bodies. He was hitting her g-spot so hard, she quickly squirted all over his cock, her entire body convulsing hard at the intense ecstasy. He kept pounding her hard, still stroking her clit, and as he shot a huge load of his cum inside her, he felt her squirt again, as she was screaming louder than he'd ever heard.

"OH FUCK. OH MIKAEL."

They sat next to each other on the couch, panting hard. Their bodies were drenched in sweat and a mixture of other fluids. After a few minutes, she heard Mikael start laughing.

"What's so funny?"

"I was just thinking about what we did."

"And that was funny?"

"No, not that, that was hot."

"Then tell me why you're laughing."

"If this was a porn, I came up with the perfect title."

"What?"

"Pet Shop Passion."

"I love that," Hannah replied, laughing.

After a quick cleanup of her office from their dirty deeds, they headed home to have some dinner. After they ate and took Cocoa for a walk, they came back and got packed up for their trip as they would be leaving in the morning. Hannah noticed Mikael had one bag already packed and secured with a lock.

"What's in there?" she asked, pointing at the bag.

"You'll find out," he said coyly.

She felt her heart start racing, as she had a feeling it was something naughty. She had a few surprises of her own hidden at the bottom of her suitcase. Once they were done packing, they decided to take a nice long soak in his tub. Mikael turned all the jets on, which felt amazing though not as amazing as what happened in her office. Thinking about that was getting her all worked up. Knowing it would drive Mikael crazy, she started pleasuring herself, moaning softly. She smiled when she saw his dick spring to life, so she moved her hand to him, stroking him lightly. She took her other hand and gently massaged his balls, as she heard him growling.

"I want you. My bed. Now!" Mikael commanded.

Hannah climbed out of the tub, dried off and laid down in bed. Mikael followed her and laid next to her.

"Wanna try something new?" he asked.

"Oooh, yes, please."

"Wrap those beautiful lips around my cock, but first, get that sexy pussy on my face."

She positioned herself, lowered her head and sucked his dick, dragging her tongue up and down, stopping to swirl around the head. After a few minutes, she felt his tongue on her clit. She moaned as sucked on him, the vibrations adding to his pleasure. She rocked back and forth from the pleasure. He took his hands and massaged her breasts, making her moan even louder. She tickled his balls with her fingers, feeling him getting close. She sucked harder and faster until her mouth was full of his salty cream, which she eagerly swallowed. He sucked her clit hard, fingers inside her stroking her g spot until she exploded in his face. She laid next to him, her head on his chest.

"Damn, that was so sexy," he said.

"Mmm. That was the first time I've ever done that. I think my new favorite number is 69," she joked.

After cleaning up their faces from their naughty fun, they headed to bed, excited to welcome the new day and their trip to Atlantic City. Mikael turned off the light, then pulled her close and kissed her tenderly.

"I love you, Hannah."

"I love you too, Mikael."

Chapter Fifteen

After dropping Cocoa and Leo off at Dean and Alex's, Mikael and Hannah started their journey to Atlantic City. When they arrived at the Hard Rock Hotel, Mikael pulled into the valet line and unloaded their luggage. As he had booked the full VIP package, a bellhop came and loaded all their bags onto a cart and took them to the VIP entrance to check in. They were escorted to their suite, where the bellhop unloaded their bags, and after Mikael tipped him, he headed out. Hannah walked around, in awe of the size of their room. She loved that they had a soaking tub, knowing there would likely be some naughty activities in there. The bedroom featured a king size bed and the living room had a beautiful sofa and a dining room table, along with a bar.

They decided to start their day with a tour of the hotel, so they could see all the different rock memorabilia displayed throughout the hotel. Hannah was going nuts, taking pictures of everything. Mikael couldn't help but laugh at how much fun she was having. They walked through the casino and headed out to the boardwalk. Despite it being October, there was still a decent crowd, but not so many people that you couldn't enjoy it. They walked from one end to the other, checking out the different shops.

It was approaching noon, so they stopped at a pizza stand. Nothing compared to boardwalk pizza. Hannah had always loved coming to the shore when she was a kid. Her step-dad would always take her off exploring, a nice break from her mom's constant put-downs. She quickly pushed her mom out of her head, and turned her focus back to her sexy man. Once they finished their pizza, they grabbed a funnel cake to share. Making sure she had Mikael's attention, she started slowly licking the powdered sugar off her fingers, keeping eye contact with him.

She could see him starting to get excited and could only imagine what was happening in those sexy jeans. When they were done with their dessert, Mikael was practically panting, watching her lick the sugar from around her lips. She flashed him a naughty smile. He got up and threw their trash away.

"Room. Now!"

Hannah smiled again at how his chest was heaving with desire when he commanded her to their room. They practically ran back to the hotel and quickly raced back to their suite. Once they were inside, Mikael turned on some music and sat down in a chair across from the bed.

"Dance for me, baby," he commanded.

Hannah started swaying her hips, as she removed her shirt. After unhooking her bra, she tossed it on the floor and ran her hands over her breasts as she kept grinding her hips seductively. Mikael ran his hand over the bulge in his jeans, licking his lips as he watched her. She turned her back to him and bent down to remove her sneakers and socks. Keeping her back to him, she slid her jeans down, revealing black lace panties. She heard Mikael emit a low growl when she slid them down, giving him a nice view of her ass. Mikael got up and gave her a smack on her naked ass. The sting of his hand quickly turned to pleasure, setting her pussy on fire.

"Lay down in the middle of the bed."

After Hannah was where he wanted her, he opened the locked bag she had seen. He walked over to the bed and put a blindfold on her. Her heart started racing with desire, anxious to feel what he would do next.

"Baby, I want to cuff your wrists and ankles to the bed. Is that okay?"

"Mmmm, yes please."

"If, at any point, you start to feel uncomfortable, just say the word."

"I want this."

She felt the mattress move as Mikael secured the restraints between that and the box spring. She then felt cuffs encircle her wrists and ankles, leaving her lying there spread eagle, completely exposed. She would never have let anyone do this to her without deep trust, something she definitely had with Mikael. He left her lying there for what felt like forever. He wasn't moving, or speaking so she had no idea where he was. She assumed he was looking at her, and that thought excited her.

Suddenly, she felt the bed move and she could feel his breath near her, but no contact. She felt him move and suddenly she felt something soft teasing the insides of her thighs. Even the slightest touch was driving her wild. She wanted nothing more than to feel his hands on her. She felt him slide what he was holding across her pussy, getting her even wetter.

"Did you like that?" he asked.

"Oh yes. What was it?"

"A feather tickler."

"Ooh, so good."

She felt the bed move and his lips crushed to hers, his tongue eagerly teasing hers. He moved down to her neck, kissing her softly. She felt his mouth around one of her breasts, his tongue flicking her nipple. He started sucking her breast hard, then repeated the same on her other breast, and she knew she was going to have hickeys. She could barely stand not feeling something touch her pussy, his tongue, his dick, his fingers. She was so hot and wet for him, she didn't care.

He trailed his tongue down between her breasts, stopping at her sexy stomach. She felt him alternating between soft kisses and little love bites and the mix of sensations had her writhing, pulling against her restraints. He was driving her absolutely crazy with desire.

As if he could read her mind, he said, "Am I making you crazy yet?"

"Oh god, yes."

"What do you want more than anything right now?"

"I want you to touch my pussy."

"Maybe if you beg."

"Please touch me. I can't take much more. I'm so fuckin' hot for you and my pussy's so wet. I want you so damn bad."

"You look so fuckin' sexy laying there like that. Now it's time for me to get a taste."

She felt his mouth cover her pussy as his tongue flicked lightly at her clit. It felt so damn good feeling his hot tongue where she most wanted it. She ached to run her fingers through his hair. She writhed as much as she could in her restraints. He was teasing her with the lightest of licks, driving her even more crazy.

"Please go harder. I need you, I crave you. I wanna feel you bite my clit."

"Holy shit, my naughty woman."

He started sucking her clit hard, along with a couple of soft bites, and a calming pleasure washed over her entire body. No man had ever made her feel like Mikael, and she loved him so much, it almost hurt. She moaned louder with each suck from those sexy lips until she was quaking as her entire body exploded with a powerful orgasm.

"Oh, Mikael, please let me feel that cock inside me."

"Oh, baby."

"First, uncuff me. I'm aching to touch you."

He got up and freed her restraints then removed her blindfold. Her eyes darted right to his sexy dick, standing at full attention. There was nothing she loved more than feeling him slide that monster inside her. He filled her like no man ever had. He got back in bed and laid on top of her, slowly, teasingly sliding his cock into her pussy. Still so sensitive from her orgasm, every thrust sent her flying. She wrapped her arms around him, pulling him close as he leaned down and kissed her mouth hard. The room was quiet, except for the sounds of two lovers, moaning as they spent the afternoon passionately making love, feeling pleasure, not just in their bodies but also in their hearts.

She felt his chest heaving hard as he approached his own release. She grabbed his hot, muscular ass, squeezing him hard, trying to pull him into her even deeper. He was groaning loudly as his thrusts intensified until he spilled his load inside her, a long, low growl coming from his gut as he felt wave after wave of ecstasy wash over his body. Hannah affected him in a way no woman had ever done, and he loved how much fun she was in bed. He moved next to her and held her tight in his arms.

Both of them starving after their hot, sexy workout, they showered then headed down to Sugar Factory for dinner.

Hannah couldn't believe her eyes when she saw the drink menu. She opted for the Peanut Butter Cup martini, while Mikael opted for a drink called Sexual Chocolate. They each ordered a burger, and holy shit, were they huge. After their sexcapades earlier, neither of them had trouble finishing. After they were done, they decided to head down to the casino and try their luck on the slot machines. They opted for penny slots, and ended up coming out about $80 ahead. Mikael loved seeing how much she was enjoying herself.

The weather outside was beautiful, a little warmer than the usual Octobers on the East Coast, so they decided to take an evening stroll on the beach. They both removed their shoes, loving the feeling of the cool sand between their toes. Mikael took her hand in his as they walked. The sky was a beautiful color as the sun was just starting his descent to make way for the moon's chance to shine. After they walked for about an hour, Mikael sat down. When Hannah sat next to him, Mikael put an arm around her shoulders, as she laid her head on his.

Sitting here watching the sun dance on the water, his beautiful woman right next to him, Mikael was the happiest he'd ever been. He gently laid her down, kissing her passionately. She wrapped her arms around him as their tongues danced seductively in each other's mouths. She could feel him starting to get hard against her. She moved her body against his, driving him even more wild.

Breathlessly, he whispered, "We need to get back to the room now!"

He stood then helped her up and they headed back to the hotel. They were pawing at each other in the elevator, barely able to wait until they got back to their room to get naked. By the time they reached the living room, there was a trail of clothes. Deciding she wanted to be in charge this time, Hannah pointed at the bar.

"Get that hot, naked ass on that bar, now!"

Mikael flashed her a naughty smile as he sat on top of the bar. Hannah walked over to him, and ran her hands through his long, brown hair. She moved down to his chest, running her hands and her tongue all over him. She moved her head down a little lower, and wrapped her mouth around his dick, as her fingers lightly teased his balls. He threw his head back, groaning loudly. She ran her tongue up and down as she sucked, stopping to swirl the head like an ice cream cone.

"Baby, that feels so good."

She felt his balls moving as he approached his orgasm. She increased the speed and pressure on his dick until she heard him groan loudly as he filled her mouth with his cum. She looked into his eyes as she swallowed him down.

"Mmmm, that's my kinda drink," she said with a wicked gleam in her eyes. "Now, lay back. Your dirty girl wants to go for a ride!"

"Holy fuckin' shit!"

Hannah got up onto the bar and slowly crawled to Mikael. She lowered herself down on his dick, hard again despite having just given her a warm, salty cocktail. She sat up straight, taking him in as deep as she could, as he wrapped his arms around her to support her. She slid her pussy up and down his cock fast and hard, wanting nothing more than to feel that ultimate release. He met her passion with strong, hard thrusts and they quickly exploded together, screaming in ecstasy, their bodies glistening with sweat as they both quivered, their bodies on fire, their hearts filled with more love than either knew was possible.

Hannah lowered herself down from the bar, followed by Mikael. He pulled her close and kissed her hard. They were both completely wired after their hot tryst.

"How about we shower then hit DAER?"

"I don't know, I'm not sure I'm hot enough for a club like that."

"The fuck you aren't. Every man in there is going to wish he was me when they see you on my arm."

Hannah smiled and blushed as she walked over to her suitcase. "Alex helped me pick this out."

She held up a short, black dress and a pair of strappy, low heels. Mikael felt his knees go weak. They got in the shower, lathering each others' bodies. Once they were done, and dried off, they got dressed. Mikael just stood there, mouth hanging open, as she sat down to put her shoes on. She cleared her throat, as she was ready and he was still standing there in just underwear.

"And they say women take forever to get ready."

"Okay, smartass. Keep that up and no more sex for you."

"You might wanna think that through."

"Good point. But, it's your fault that I'm not ready."

"I beg your pardon."

"That dress, that body, those heels, holy shit, baby."

Hannah turned about ten shades of red, as Mikael laughed. He quickly got dressed in leather pants and a black button-down shirt. He left half the buttons open, showing off the sexy chest hair that drove her wild. He took her arm and linked it through his then they headed to the elevator. They were the only ones in there, so they kissed the whole time. They walked up to the doors of the club. The bouncer at the door recognized Mikael and grabbed his cell and dialed, putting the phone on speaker.

"Boss, we have a VIP."

"Who?"

"Mikael Alfredsson."

"How many in his party?"

"Two."

"Bring them to the VIP area."

All eyes were on them as they were escorted upstairs to a table with plush, leather chairs. Their escort pulled Hannah's chair out then did the same for Mikael. He headed out and a few minutes later, a waiter came in and took their drink orders. This was Hannah's first time in a club like this. They had their club in Lancaster, but that was nowhere near the level of this place. They even had a private bathroom here. She figured Mikael, however, had seen his fair share of them.

"You must be used to places like this," Hannah said.

"Yeah, but it's nice to be able to share it with someone."

"What do you mean?"

"I tried to never take Liza with me. She was too rude to the waitstaff."

"I'm sorry you had to deal with someone like her."

"It's all good now. I'm with the hottest woman here."

"I love you."

"I love you too."

The waiter returned with their drinks. Hannah smiled and thanked him, as Mikael handed him a tip. After a quick toast, they both finished their drinks. Mikael stood and put his hand out.

"Let's dance."

"Okay."

Hannah stood and Mikael pulled her in close, as their bodies moved along with the beat from that night's amazing DJ. She looked up and Mikael and saw his eyes were firmly planted on the cleavage spilling out of her dress. It turned her on when he looked at her like that, and she started grinding against him.

He whispered in her ear, "Bathroom! Now!"

He took her hand and let her to the huge private bathroom, then closed and locked the door. He pointed to the counter next to the sink and she walked over. He turned her around and stood behind her. She watched in the mirror as he removed his pants, freeing his erection. He lifted her dress and removed her black lace panties. She felt him enter her pussy from behind as she held the counter for support. He held her hips as he pounded her hard and fast, hitting her g-spot with every thrust.

She never thought she would, but she loved seeing their reflection in the mirror as they fucked. He moved a hand around and started rubbing her clit. He felt so fucking good that she quickly lost all control and she exploded, soaking his dick. He quickly followed, mixing his fluid with hers. Both of their faces were red matching the heat of that incredible fuck. They got dressed and headed back to their table where fresh drinks were waiting for them. They quickly finished them then headed down to the main floor and danced until the wee hours of the morning.

Chapter Sixteen

They awoke mid-morning and ordered room service for breakfast. After they showered and dressed, Mikael had a surprise for Hannah.

"I booked us something special for this morning."

"What?"

"An appointment at the Rock Spa & Salon. The package I ordered is called 'Your Body is a Wonderland.' We get to paint each other with mud, then relax in a tub for two, and end our session with a couples massage."

"Oh my god. I totally don't deserve this."

"Yes you do. We do. I love you."

"I love you so much."

When it came time to head down, they walked hand-in-hand to the elevator, kissing the entire way down. They headed into the spa and were taken to the couples suite. The room was so beautiful and peaceful. Their therapist explained everything to them, got their bath ready, then left the room. She let them know that a chime would ring to let them know the massage would begin shortly, so they would have ample time to finish their bath in private.

Mikael walked over to Hannah and removed her clothes, caressing her skin as he exposed her. She returned the favor then grabbed the mud and started painting him. When she was done, he did the same for her. They got in the tub, Mikael sitting with his back against the tub and Hannah in front of him, leaning back against his chest. He wrapped his arms around her and held her close as they closed their eyes, enjoying the warm, relaxing bath. The water was infused with Himalayan salt, juniper berry and geranium, which felt and smelled amazing.

Hannah felt his hands start moving down her belly, getting closer to the spot she most loved feeling him. He teased all around her mound, but never made contact, which drove her even more crazy. She vowed to make him pay later, though she had a feeling he wouldn't object to what she had planned. She turned her head slightly so she could reach his lips and kissed him hard, eagerly sliding her tongue into his mouth, just enough to leave him wanting more. A few minutes later, the chime rang, so they got out of the tub and dried off, and put on the robes that were left for them.

They each laid on the massage tables, removed their robes and covered themselves with towels. The therapists entered the room and gave them the most amazing massage they'd ever felt. They turned their heads, gazing into each others' eyes the entire time. Once they were done, the therapists left them so they could get dressed. Mikael pulled her in close and kissed her passionately, his strong hands on her back. She reached down and grabbed two handfuls of that hot ass of his.

"This was amazing. I've never been pampered like that before. Thank you," she said.

"It was my pleasure."

"It will be," she said, a naughty smile appearing on her face.

They got dressed and headed back to the room. Mikael couldn't stop thinking about what Hannah had said after their massage and wondered what she had in store for him. He was already excited for later. The concert was going to be a blast and he was so excited they would be meeting the band after the show. Hannah disappeared into the bedroom then he heard her go into the bathroom. A few minutes later, he heard a whistle blow from the bedroom. He walked in to see what was going on, and his jaw dropped to the floor. Hannah stood there in a referee's uniform that left little to the imagination.

"I'm calling a penalty on you," she said in a voice so sultry that his dick strained against his pants.

"What did I do?"

"Teasing me in the tub earlier."

"How so?"

"By not touching me where I most wanted you."

"What's my penalty?"

"Get your ass on that bed! NOW!"

He laid on the bed and watched as she slid her shorts off, giving him a view of her beautiful lower half. She joined him on the bed and he felt his breath catch in his throat at the sight of that delicious woman. She got on her knees, facing the wall and braced her hands on the pillowy headboard.

"Get that hot mouth on my pussy and make me scream."

He positioned himself so his head was between her legs. He covered her entire mound with his mouth and slid his tongue inside her, licking hard. She started moaning softly. He moved his tongue to her clit, swollen with desire, and flicked it with his tongue as her moaning got louder. He started sucking hard on her clit and felt her body starting to quiver as she moved closer to orgasm. She started bucking on his face as she exploded in orgasm.

Mikael didn't let up and kept licking and sucking her. She reached orgasm quicker and quicker each time. Still, he wouldn't stop, loving the feeling of her entire body quaking. He was so fucking hard that his dick practically ripped through his pants. She tried to move off him, but he had a hold of her hips.

"So good. I can't take much more."

He ignored her and kept sucking on her, adding a couple of fingers inside her, stroking her g-spot so hard that she squirted on his face. Her skin was on fire, drenched in sweat, shaking hard with pleasure. She slid down his body and opened his jeans and lowered herself on his dick, her pussy so wet from her multiple orgasms that he slid in with ease. She rode him hard, so sensitive that she quickly exploded again. He was so turned on, he quickly followed, filling her with the salty cream she loved so much. She rolled off and laid next to him, both of them so spent, they quickly fell asleep.

After a nice hour-long nap, they got up and shared a hot steamy shower. After getting dressed, they headed down to dinner before the concert. As they were dressed in jeans and t-shirts for the concert, they opted for one of the casual dining restaurants in the hotel, Hard Rock Cafe. After they ate, they went outside to the boardwalk for a nice evening walk. They stopped on a bench and kissed for a while before heading back inside to go to the concert.

They were escorted down to the first row. Hannah sat there, awestruck at how close they were. She was excited enough to be seeing her favorite band, as she'd never before had the chance. Seeing them this close, and then getting to meet them afterwards had her mesmerized. The best part of all, though, was being here with Mikael. She loved him so much. About half an hour after they were in their seats, the opening act came on. Hannah was getting more and more excited as she got closer to seeing her heroes.

Once the stage was ready, the intro the band always used started and Hannah felt tears start rolling down her face. She was so beyond excited that she couldn't control her emotions. Mikael looked over and saw her, pulling her close as the curtain dropped and the band appeared on stage. Hannah was screaming and cheering loudly. She and Mikael danced through the entire show. Once the show was done and the band left the stage, everyone screamed and yelled for an encore, which they always did, much to the delight of the crowd.

A few minutes later, they returned to the stage for a few more songs. During their last song, they shot off confetti guns and ribbon guns, covering the crowd. It was amazing, and Hannah was so grateful she got to experience this with the love of her life.

"So, what did you think, better than the other times you'd seen them?" Mikael asked.

"It was one of the best nights of my life," she gushed.

"It's not over yet. Ready to meet them?"

"No but yes."

"You'll be fine," Mikael laughed.

He took her hand as they headed to the VIP area. Once security confirmed their passes, they were taken to a room where the meet and greet would take place. Mikael could see Hannah getting nervous, so he put a hand on her shoulder.

"Don't be nervous, they're dudes just like me."

"I can't help it."

"Let's go get in line."

Hannah smiled nervously as they took their place in line. They were fairly close to the front, so they only had to wait a little while. When it was their turn, they were taken inside where the band was sitting at a table. The band's manager handed them each a poster to have signed. Hannah was so starstruck she could barely speak, so Mikael did most of the talking. After the autographs were done, they had a photo taken with the band. Hannah got to stand between the guitarist and the drummer, her two favorite members. She couldn't stop smiling.

Because Mikael was also a famous musician, he was invited to stay for the after-party, something he hadn't told Hannah about. She couldn't believe she was going to be at an intimate gathering with this amazing group of guys. Once the regular meet and greet was over, the venue staff brought in some champagne and hors d'oeuvres for everyone. Mikael grabbed a glass each for himself and Hannah. They slowly sipped their delicious bubbly treat. The food smelled great, but Hannah was too nervous to eat.

Her knees buckled when the band's drummer approached her and she had to grab onto Mikael to keep from going down. After a couple minutes of chatting with Mikael, he asked her what her name was and to her surprise, she actually remembered. He smiled and chatted with her, making her feel more comfortable. By the time she met the rest of the band, she was herself again, impressing Mikael with how easily she talked with them. Once the after-party was done, they headed to the casino to try their luck.

Hannah liked playing the penny slots, so she didn't lose a lot. They found a couple of open machines, and much to their surprise, found they were hot. When they cashed out, they were about $100 ahead. Mikael heard Hannah yawn.

"Tired, babe?" he asked.

"A bit, after today's activities, but I don't want to go back to the room."

"Come with me."

They walked over to the Starbucks that was in the hotel and ordered coffees, hoping it would wake them up a little bit. After downing a super-sweet treat, Hannah was wired, so they headed to DAER. This time, they didn't go into the VIP part and headed right to the dance floor. Hannah loved dancing in Mikael's arms. A slower song came on, so he pulled her close, kissing her tenderly as they swayed together. They walked over to the bar to grab a drink and a little something to eat. They finished up then returned to the dance floor, staying until the club closed then headed to their suite.

They were alone in the elevator, so Mikael pulled her in close and kissed her hard, jamming his tongue in her mouth. He pushed the button to stop the elevator then turned and gave her the naughtiest look she'd ever seen.

"Get against the wall, you sexy minx," he commanded.

Hannah stood against the wall. Mikael walked over and turned her around so she was facing it. He slid her jeans and panties down then spread her legs. He stood behind her and freed his erection, sliding inside her pussy from behind. She braced her hands on the wall as she felt him pound her hard.

"Oh fuck, baby, it feels so good inside you."

"Oh Mikael, fuck me harder," she cried out.

His thrusts became more powerful as his breathing increased until she felt him empty himself inside her. He moved his fingers to her clit, and she exploded with her own powerful climax, the elevator wall keeping her from collapsing to the ground. They quickly pulled their clothes back on and Mikael restarted the elevator. She had to hold on to him, her legs still shaking from her orgasm. He threw her over his shoulder and carried her the rest of the way to the room, feeling her hands firmly planted on his ass. He put her down when they got inside.

"Thank you so much for everything tonight," she said, wrapping her arms around him.

"My pleasure," he said with a naughty wink.

Both of them exhausted from an action-packed day, they headed to bed and quickly fell into a deep sleep.

Chapter Seventeen

Hannah was lulled from her slumber by the delicious aroma of coffee and bacon. She sleepily floated out to the suite's living room, her eyes treated to the sight of her man sitting there in nothing but black silk boxers. Hannah felt a couple drops of drool roll out of her mouth, which she quickly wiped away. She walked over to her sexy lover and kissed him hard. She felt some activity in those silky boxers.

"Well, well, it appears the snake is awake," she joked.

"Thanks to you."

"Mmmm."

"Are you hungry?"

"Oh, yes," she said, looking down her lashes at him.

"Down, girl," he quipped.

"What, you can't handle this," she said, sweeping her hands like a game show model

"So, that's how you want to play?"

Mikael threw her over his shoulder and carried her to bed. He quickly stripped off the lace nightie she was wearing, his eyes drinking in her exquisite curves.

"Fuck, you're so sexy," he said.

"Then come take me, stud."

MIkael slid his boxers down, showing Hannah his fully erect, delicious cock. He climbed on top of her and swiftly slid inside her. They fucked hard and fast, both of them quickly exploding together. Now completely famished, they headed back to the dining area to enjoy breakfast. When they were done, they grabbed showers then headed out to the boardwalk. Hannah found that people-watching was quickly becoming a favorite pastime. The boardwalk sure did feature its share of interesting characters. They were sitting on a bench, enjoying the scent of the ocean and the cool, fall breeze behind them.

"I have a special night planned for our last night here," Mikael said.

"Ooooh, what?"

"It's a surprise."

"I love it."

"How do you know when it hasn't happened yet?"

"Because I love everything we do together."

Mikael caressed her cheek and kissed her tenderly. She sighed contentedly as she laid her head on his strong shoulder. As lunchtime was rolling around, they decided to walk along the boardwalk and find a pizza stand. They grabbed a table and enjoyed a slice and a funnel cake.

"Wanna go check out the carnival games?" Hannah asked.

"Let's go," Mikael said excitedly.

They spent the afternoon battling each other in every game the carnival had to offer, most of which Hannah won. She had a feeling it wasn't because she was better, but she didn't care. They were having a blast, laughing and carrying on like teenagers. They were so wrapped up in the fun, they never saw the man watching them. Mikael was carrying the rather large stuffed elephant Hannah won, his eyes as bright as the sun with love for this incredible woman.

They stopped at a bench along the boardwalk and did a little more people-watching. The Atlantic City boardwalk certainly featured more than its share of crazy characters. Hannah was having fun making up backstories on some of them. One in particular stuck with her. She saw a woman holding onto her man as they walked. She was clad in denim shorts that barely covered her ass, a tight tank top and heels that she couldn't walk in. High heels are a bad idea on the boardwalk to begin with, especially when you can't handle walking in them. The man appeared to have money, and Hannah figured he was forcing her to dress that way, as she seemed quite uncomfortable.

"We need to head back to the room and get ready," Mikael said.

"I'm so excited," Hannah replied.

They went back up to the room to get ready. They took a long steamy shower together then got dressed. Hannah saw a box on the bed with a big bow on it.

"Is that for me?"

"Yes, baby."

She walked over and opened the box. She picked up the most beautiful yellow dress she'd ever seen. It was a short-sleeved, satin dress that went to the floor. There was also a pair of yellow flats in the box.

"This is stunning," she said.

"Ever since I saw you in those beautiful yellow dresses at Alex and Dean's rehearsal dinner and wedding, I have loved that color. I recruited Alex to help me."

"Thank you so much."

"Can't wait to see it on you."

Hannah loved the way the dress felt on her skin. She looked over at Mikael, who was just standing there with his mouth hanging open, gawking at her. He made a mental note to thank Alex for her help. He grabbed his phone and snapped a photo of his gorgeous woman. He got dressed in a white cotton button down shirt and khakis, along with casual shoes. He stood next to Hannah and took a selfie of them. It was clear from the photo that they were made for each other.

A little before six, there was a knock on their door.

"Sir, your dinner reservation is ready," Hannah heard the bellhop say.

Mikael walked over to Hannah and linked her arm through his. The bellhop led them to the elevator, and escorted them to the beach. Hannah saw a part of the beach roped off. Inside the rope was a small cafe table and two chairs. They walked over to the table and sat down. Shortly after, a waiter appeared with wine and two glasses. He poured them each a glass then headed back inside. They clinked glasses and each took a sip. A few minutes later, another waiter appeared with their food.

A plate of spaghetti and meatballs was placed in front of each of them, along with two salads and a basket of garlic bread. After confirming everything was to their liking, the waiter left them to eat.

"I asked Alex what your favorite movie was and she told me you always loved 'Lady and the Tramp'," Mikael said.

He pulled out his phone, and turned on the song that was playing in the scene when the dogs are eating the same meal she was about to enjoy.

"Oh my god, I can't believe you did this. I love you," Hannah said, tears filling her beautiful eyes.

"I love you," Mikael responded.

Once they had finished eating, the waiter who served them came and cleaned up the food then removed the table and chairs. He nodded at Mikael.

"How about a moonlight stroll?" Mikael asked.

"I'd love too."

They removed their shoes, feeling the cool sand between their toes. They walked, holding hands, down the beach, almost deserted as night was approaching. After about an hour, they headed back to where their table had been. Hannah's eyes went wide when she saw a cabana set up. She looked over at Mikael, and noticed a naughty gleam in his gorgeous blue eyes. They walked inside the cabana and were greeted by a beautiful king-sized canopy bed, complete with red satin sheets.

"Oh, Mikael," was all Hannah could muster.

"Are you happy?"

"More than you could ever imagine."

Mikael pulled her close, kissing her passionately. She loved the feeling of his tongue exploring her mouth, as she intertwined her tongue with his, Like always, she felt that oh-so-familiar heat building between her thighs. She couldn't help but notice she wasn't the only one who was excited. He unzipped her dress, letting it fall to the ground, leaving her standing there in her white lace bra and panties.

"So beautiful, baby," he said as he unhooked her bra and let it fall on top of the dress.

He hooked his fingers underneath her panties and slid them down. He looked down as he felt her start to unbutton his shirt, running her hands on his chest as she finished removing it. Her smile widened when she moved her hand to his pants and removed them, noting that he wasn't wearing any underwear. She looked down at his erection and moaned softly, anticipating what he was planning to do to her tonight.

"Come lay in bed with me," he said softly.

While she loved when he commanded her in the bedroom, she also loved this softer side of him. She joined him in bed, the satin sheets feeling amazing on her skin, but not nearly as amazing as Mikael did. The cool ocean breeze swept across their naked bodies and Hannah shivered as the chill hit her skin. Mikael leaned on top of her and kissed her, tenderly at first, but quickly increasing in passion as he ran his hand down her body. She wrapped her arms around him and pulled him closer, loving the warmth of his naked skin.

He kissed her neck then slid his tongue between her breasts, stopping to suck each one, his tongue flicking her hard nipples. He felt her writhe and moan at his touch. He trailed his tongue down her beautiful stomach and showered her with soft kisses. He slid a couple fingers inside her and felt her desire for him.

"Baby, you're so wet."

"Mmmm, I want you."

Purposely skipping her eager core, he made his way down each leg, licking and sucking the insides of her thighs, driving her insane. He knew what she wanted, but he wanted this to last. He worked his way back up her body until his lips were on hers. She eagerly joined her tongue to his, moaning into his mouth. She raised her bottom off the bed, desperate to be touched in her most intimate of areas. Mikael took another tour down her body with his mouth, this time stopping between her legs.

She felt his tongue lightly caress her swollen clit and she responded with a soft moan. He increased the pressure with each stroke of his tongue which she matched with louder moans. He slid his tongue between her folds, licking her hard, lapping up her sweet honey as she writhed beneath him. He felt her body starting to quiver, so he stopped touching her, wanting to prolong their lovemaking.

"Oh god, please don't stop," she cried out.

Mikael looked at her with a wickedness in his eyes.

"You need to convince me to continue."

"Please, Mikael. I want you so fuckin' bad. I'm so close to exploding and need that tongue back in my pussy. Please make me come, baby."

He sucked her clit hard as he felt her entire body start to shake.

"Oh fuck, oh Mikael, so fuckin' incredible."

"What do want now, baby?"

"I need you inside me."

Mikael slid up her body and slid his dick inside her. Fuck, she felt so good. He held her tight, kissing her softly, as he slowly and gently moved inside her. He loved the feeling of her arms around him, hands running over his back. Her soft skin and her body felt incredible when they made love. The sounds of their lovemaking combined with the waves lightly crashing on the shore was like something out of a movie. They spent the next several hours loving each other until they had nothing left. They climbed under the covers and quickly fell asleep, holding each other close.

They were awakened the following morning by the sun shining into their cabana. Hannah woke up and stretched, completely sated from the night of passion she and Mikael shared. She nestled back into his arms as he stirred awake. He kissed her tenderly, loving the feeling of waking up next to her. He never wanted to know a morning that she wasn't by his side. He grabbed his phone.

"What would you like for breakfast?" he asked.

With a wicked smile, she answered, "You."

"Damn, woman!"

"Seriously, though, I'd love a Belgian waffle and coffee."

Mikael dialed the hotel and ordered breakfast. They got up and dressed while they waited for the food to be delivered. After they ate, they headed back inside the hotel to pack up and head back to reality. At least her reality still included having this incredible man by her side. After they checked out, Mikael thanked the concierge for accommodating his requests and handed him what must have been a sizable gratuity, given the way his face lit up. He called for the valet to bring Mikael's truck around and escorted them to the waiting area. As they headed home, they laughed and talked, reliving all the fun they'd just had. Once they arrived at Hannah's house, Mikael helped her unload her stuff.

"What are your plans today?" Mikael asked.

"Gonna shower then head down to the shop. I need to start getting the Halloween decorations set up."

"After I unpack and shower, I'll come down and help with whatever you need."

"Thank you and especially thank you for this trip."

"My pleasure, babe," he said then walked over and gave her a warm hug and tender kiss goodbye.

Hannah called Alex before she headed out so she could pick up Cocoa and Leo then she went to her shop. Kurt was busy with some customers, so he just gave her a quick wave. She walked up to the counter to give him a hand. Once they finished with all the customers, he updated her on what happened while she was gone. Luckily, other than being a little busy, things went smoothly. Hannah was about to head to her office when she saw Eden walk in. Hannah walked over and greeted her.

"How's business going?" Hannah asked.

"Things are starting to pick up. I did come to ask for your help, though."

"What can I do?"

"Would you be open to me providing the food for your Halloween event?"

"I would love that. For one, it would save me having to worry about that part, plus I'm happy to help you get more traffic. I usually have good participation so that will drive more business your way."

"Thank you so much."

"Of course, we all need to help support each other. I was just getting ready to update the signs for this year, so I'll add you to it. Do you want to take a look and approve it before I print them?"

"No need, I trust you."

"Sounds great."

Eden waved and headed back to her shop, so Hannah went to her office to get the signs ready. Mikael got to the store a few minutes later, so Kurt let him know she was in her office. He knocked on the door and asked, "You decent?"

"Yes, fully clothed," she laughed.

"I can change that."

"Get that sexy ass in here."

Mikael walked inside, leaned down and kissed her hard. She playfully pushed him away.

"I'm trying to work."

"Fine. I'll help you work now, but we're gonna play later."

Mikael helped her get the store decorated for Halloween and get the signs ready to hang. He took one across the street for Eden to hang in her window. He noticed a man standing on the corner looking in the direction of Hannah's shop. He wondered if they knew each other. When he saw Mikael looking his way, he headed into the restaurant. When Mikael went into the restaurant, he saw the man talking to Eden. He handed her the sign then went back to Hannah's shop and hung out with her until closing time. They stopped for hoagies on the way to Mikael's house.

After they finished eating and taking Cocoa for a quick walk, Mikael grabbed a deck of cards and motioned for Hannah to join him at the kitchen table.

"I told you we were going to play. Up for some strip Texas Hold 'Em?" Mikael asked.

Hannah had to fight a smile at how smug Mikael was looking. If only he knew she watched the World Series of Poker religiously and had been studying the game for years. She was going to show him. Mikael dealt the first hand, which Hannah played as if she'd never seen a deck of cards before. She purposely lost the first few hands, losing both shoes and both socks. She saw Mikael getting more cocky, so she knew it was time for him to find out how fierce a competitor she was.

Hannah never lost another piece of clothing. Across the table from her, Mikael was down to his briefs. Hannah's expression gave nothing away. She peeked at her hole cards and saw a two and a seven, the worst hand in poker. Despite that, she bluffed her way to getting Mikael to fold pocket queens. His jaw dropped when she flipped over her cards.

"What the hell?"

"I've been watching poker on ESPN for as long as I can remember. Now, get up and let's see the goods," she said with a huge grin on her face.

Mikael removed his underwear and was met with whistles and

catcalls from his naughty woman. He couldn't believe how badly she had just played him. Hannah was dancing around the room, gloating at her victory. Mikael walked over and tried to hug her.

"No, no, no. I won, so I'm in charge tonight. Now, get that hot, naked body in the bedroom."

She followed him in, got naked and laid down on the bed, spreading her legs wide. She was still gloating with a very smug look on her face after kicking his ass at poker.

She flashed him her naughtiest look and said, "You thought sure you could beat me, didn't you?"

"I sure did," he admitted sheepishly.

"Instead of making you eat crow, get your ass over here and eat my pussy. I wanna come all over your face."

Mikael licked and sucked her pussy hard until he entire body was shaking as she exploded in an extremely intense orgasm. She pushed him on his back, climbed on top and rode him hard, until she felt him empty himself inside her. She sped up her pace until another powerful climax rocked her body to its core, as she screamed at the top of her lungs. Completely spent, they quickly fell asleep and didn't wake until morning.

Chapter Eighteen

H annah woke up early the morning of her shop's Halloween party. Mikael was still asleep, so she left him a note and headed out. She loved the ride to work, especially this time of year, seeing all the houses decorated with pumpkins, ghosts, and so many other symbols of fall. She pulled into the parking lot then walked across to Eden's cafe to see if she needed help. Eden smiled when she saw Hannah's costume.

"You look adorable," Eden complimented.

"Thanks. I've loved Raggedy Ann since I was a little girl."

Once they had her stuff all set up, Hannah walked back over and opened her shop. Kurt arrived a little while later, dressed as Raggedy Andy like they had planned. They got everything done ahead of the start of the parade, so they headed over to Eden's to grab a quick bite before the festivities started. Hannah walked outside and saw that the local police were setting up barricades to close the road for the party. She heard a familiar bark, turned, and saw Cocoa in her dinosaur costume dragging Mikael toward her. She walked over and commanded Cocoa to heel. She took the leash from Mikael, laughing at how easily Cocoa was able to pull Mr. Strong and Sexy.

"Not funny," he pouted.

"Awww, poor Mikael," she quipped.

He pulled her close and kissed her hard.

"Get a room," they heard a male voice yell.

They turned and saw Dean and Alex headed their way with Holly, who was dressed as a superhero.

"Forgive my smartass husband," Alex joked.

"Hey! Not nice," Dean replied.

They all walked over to Eden's table so the dogs could get a treat. Both girls sat, waiting patiently for Eden to give them each one of the biscuits she baked. Hannah noticed a very handsome man standing with Eden. After introducing Alex to Eden, she asked who he was.

"Who's the hottie?" Hannah asked.

"He's my head cook. His name's Max and we've been friends since high school."

"Wow! Handsome and a good cook, nice combo! Thanks for the treats."

After the dogs had their treats, Hannah and Alex rejoined their men and they headed over to the pet store.

"Can we talk for a couple minutes?" Alex whispered.

"Sure, we can go to my office," Hannah responded.

"Thanks, can you just make it like it was your idea your idea?"

"Okay."

Hannah wrinkled her brow for a second, then said, "Hey, Alex, I gotta show you the new ad campaign I'm designing for the shop. It's in my office."

Turning to Dean, Alex said, "Be back soon."

They both sat down in Hannah's office.

"What's going on?" Hannah asked.

"A couple of my friends turned on me," Alex said, tears filling her eyes.

"What happened?"

"They said they felt ignored while I was on tour with Dean."

"Sounds like they're jealous. If they can't be happy for your success, they weren't true friends."

Alex's face crumbled and she buried her head in her hands. Hannah walked over, sat down next to her, and put an arm around her shoulders. Alex laid her head on Hannah's shoulder.

"Maybe I deserve this."

"Like hell you do. You're an amazing musician and I couldn't be more proud of what you achieved. Don't let a couple of bitter bitches take that away from you."

"Thank you. I couldn't bring myself to tell Dean."

"Why?"

"I didn't want to take away from his happiness."

"You're his wife. I guarantee you're way more important to him than anything. You need to tell him, sweetie."

"Would you mind if we borrowed your office?"

"Of course not. I'll send him back."

Hannah headed out front and told Dean that Alex needed to talk to him. She took Holly's leash from him and he headed back. A little while later, they emerged. Hannah saw a huge smile on Alex's face, which made her heart happy. She handed Holly's leash to Alex. She and Dean took Holly outside to join the parade of dogs.

"What was that all about?" Mikael inquired.

"I'll fill you in later. For now, let's go have Cocoa join the parade."

Mikael took her hand as they walked outside and lead the parade of dogs. The crowd that gathered cheered as all the dogs pranced by, each looking amazing in their costumes. The event was a rousing success again this year. Hannah loved seeing the joy on everyone's faces. She walked over to Eden to see how she made out, delighted to find out that she had sold completely out of human and canine goodies.

"Thank you for allowing me to be part of this," Eden said.

"It was my pleasure. We small business owners all need to support each other. I hope this helps drive more business to your cafe."

"Me too. I need to go clean up. Thanks again."

"You're welcome."

Hannah, Mikael, Dean, and Alex headed back to Hannah's store.

"You guys going to the costume party at the club tonight?" Dean asked.

Mikael looked at Hannah. "Wanna go?"

"Sounds like fun," Hannah responded.

"Great, I'll reserve us a table," Alex added.

Dean and Alex headed out, leaving just Mikael and Hannah in the store.

"We need to go get costumes for tonight. I don't want to wear this one to the club," Hannah said.

"You already have one."

"I do?"

"Hell yeah, that sexy cop outfit."

"I can't wear that."

"Why not? You look so fuckin' hot."

"Yeah right."

"Yeah you do. Please, babe."

"I suppose. But, what about you?"

"I can be your prisoner. I saw a striped jailbird costume at the Halloween shop."

"Love it. I'll take Cocoa home if you want to go grab it."

"Sounds like a plan. Do you want to get dressed at my house or should I pick you up?"

"I guess pick me up."

He kissed her goodbye and headed out, while she closed up the shop and went home to shower and get ready. She couldn't believe she would be letting anyone else see her in that outfit. She got dressed and checked herself in the mirror. She had to admit that she didn't hate what she saw. She grabbed her accessories and waited inside for Mikael to get there. When she saw him, she put on a long coat and walked outside.

"That coat stays in the car when we get there," Mikael said.

"I guess," Hannah sighed.

They rode to the club, an awkward silence filling the car. When they arrived, Hannah removed the coat and took a deep breath.

"Let's get this over with."

"You're gorgeous, it's gonna be fine. I see Dean's car, so let's go."

They walked inside and every single pair of eyes went to Hannah. The jaw of every man they passed hit the floor. Dean and Alex had their backs to them when they approached the table. Mikael put his finger to his lips. When he was right behind Dean, he leaned near his ear.

"You gotta help me escape," Mikael pleaded.

Dean turned around and his jaw dropped. All he could muster was, "Hot damn."

Alex turned to see what he was looking at and did a double-take.

"Hannah?" she inquired. "Damn, girl."

Hannah's face brightened.

"My sexy woman," Mikael bragged.

Hannah blushed, a big smile on her face. A couple minutes later, a waiter stopped by and took their food and drink order. Mikael couldn't take his eyes off Hannah and was finding it difficult to keep his pants from tenting. He wanted her so damn bad, he could taste it. He took a couple of deep breaths, calming himself down, at least for now. Once their order arrived, that at least gave him something else to focus on. After they finished eating, both couples headed out to the dance floor. Hannah was an awesome dancer, and she sure knew how to work those sexy curves. Alex was equally as good, and all eyes were on them. Hannah looked over at their men and laughed.

"Look at those goofy grins," she joked to Alex.

Alex looked over and saw both guys just standing there gaping at them. "Follow my lead."

Alex started swirling her hips in the sexiest dance Hannah had ever seen. She nodded to Hannah, who mimicked her moves. She took Hannah's hand as they danced, each of them working their hips and ass hard. Mikael and Dean stood frozen, mouths wide open. Hannah slowly bent down pretending to adjust her boot, giving Mikael full view of her ass, laughing as she saw him wipe drool off his face. When the song ended, they returned to the table. Mikael and Dean finally figured out how to move and joined them, neither one able to speak.

They ended up staying until closing time. Hannah and Alex drank more than their fair share of beer and every stint on the dance floor got naughtier and naughtier. By the time they were all ready to head out, neither woman could walk without stumbling. Dean and Mikael left them in the care of the club's owner so they could pull their trucks up to the front. They each carried their woman out and put them in the passenger seat.

"These two are going to feel great in the morning," Dean joked.

"I bet they'll be up for a lot of sun and loud music," Mikael quipped.

Mikael drove to Hannah's house and carried her inside. He got her out of her costume and laid her down in bed.

"Play with my kitty-cat. She very wet and wanna have a thingy inside," Hannah slurred.

I think we'll save that for tomorrow," Mikael replied.

"Wanna play now, stop being a poopy-parter."

Mikael removed his costume and went to the bathroom to get ready. By the time he returned, Hannah had passed out cold. He pulled the covers up and turned out the lights, quickly falling asleep himself.

Hannah was still sound asleep when Mikael woke up. He showered, dressed and took care of Cocoa. He had just put the coffee on when he heard her stirring. Deciding to teach her a lesson, he walked into her bedroom and pulled all the curtains wide open.

"Good Morning, Sunshine," he shouted.

"Too loud, too bright,' she whispered.

"Guess you shouldn't have drank so much," he yelled.

"Hate you right now," she grumbled.

"You'll feel better after coffee and food."

"Need to shower. Need help."

Mikael laughed as he carried her to the bathroom. He helped her get undressed and waited while she showered. She looked a little better when she got out. He wrapped her in a towel and helped her back to the bedroom so she could get dressed. She shuffled into the kitchen a little while later, dressed in a t-shirt and sweatpants. She plopped down in a chair and laid her head on the table. Mikael put a cup of coffee in front of her.

"Shhh," she hissed.

A few minutes later, he laid a plate with eggs and toast on it in front of her. She wrinkled her nose and pushed it away.

"I know it doesn't feel like it, but you need to eat."

"Fork is too loud," she complained.

Mikael smirked and handed her a plastic fork.

"Will that work or do you need a paper one?"

"Ha ha, dickhead."

Hannah managed to finish her breakfast then she went and laid on the couch. She was grateful she didn't have to open the shop today, as she could barely stand having her eyes open. Mikael walked over with a cup of water and two aspirin, which she sat up and took. He sat on the floor next to her and put a warm washcloth on her forehead. A couple of tears slid down her cheeks.

"The pain?" he asked.

"No. I've never had anyone care for me like this."

"I love you."

"I love you more."

A couple minutes later, Mikael heard soft snoring next to him. He pulled a blanket over her and put the cloth in the sink. He left her a note in case she woke up then took Cocoa for a walk. As he was walking, his cell rang. He saw Dean's name on the screen and answered. Dean told him Alex wasn't doing much better than Hannah. They had a quick laugh but both of them felt bad that their women were suffering.

Hannah was still sleeping when Mikael got home, so he sat back down on the floor next to her, gazing at her as she slept. He knew one thing for certain; he wanted to spend the rest of his life taking care of her. He laid his head on the couch, and quickly dozed off himself. About an hour later, Mikael was awakened by Hannah stirring on the couch. She sat up and stretched out her arms.

"Are you feeling any better?"

"A lot. Don't let me drink that much again, please," she pleaded.

"I promise."

"I'm not sure I want to know the answer to this but what did I do?"

"Well, first of all, Alex was equally as drunk, so you weren't alone. The two of you gave the crowd quite a thrill."

"How?"

"Some of the naughtiest dancing I've ever seen."

Hannah's face turned beet red for a minute then she started laughing.

"Did it get you hot?"

"Oh yes it did, but nothing happened. You drunkenly begged me when we got home."

"And you resisted me?"

"I love having sex with you, but I would never take advantage like that."

"But now that I'm completely sober..."

Mikael scooped her up carried her to the bedroom. That was the last time either of them would be dressed for the rest of the day.

The next morning, Hannah woke up refreshed after a great night's sleep. That quickly evaporated when she got to work. Kurt woke up with a terrible cold and stayed home, which of course meant the shop would be at it's busiest. She never even had a chance to stop for food. When she finally slowed down about an hour before closing time, she called Mikael.

"You sound annoyed," he observed when he answered her call.

"It was the day from hell," she exasperated.

"What happened?"

"Kurt woke up sick and had to stay home so of course it was the busiest day ever. Then some kid threw up his guts and it still smells in here."

"Sounds like a night in with pizza and Netflix is in order."

"That may not even help. Listen, I gotta go, gonna take me a bit longer to clean. See you later."

"Love you, babe."

"Love you."

When Hannah finally finished up, she was exhausted and cranky. All she wanted to do was go home and get in her jammies. She listened to some of Mikael's music on the way home, but even that didn't do much for her food. When she got inside, she didn't see Mikael. All of a sudden, she swore she could hear yodeling. That's it, I've flipped my lid, she thought to herself.

"I'm home," she called out.

"Coming," Mikael yelled back.

As he walked out toward the living room, she swore the yodeling was getting louder. She shook her head, but she could still hear it. She sat down at the kitchen table and bent forward, head in her hands. She suddenly saw a pair of furry bear feet. The yodeling was also even louder.

"Look at me, baby," he commanded.

Hannah looked up and almost choked. Mikael was standing there in a pair of boxers with a plastic dill pickle sticking out of them. She started laughing so hard, she couldn't breathe. When she finally managed to control herself, she stood up, and grabbed his pickle.

"What the hell?"

"It was a gag gift from Dean a couple years back. When you told me how your day went, I wanted to try to cheer you up."

"That sure as hell did it. Thank you."

"Happy to help. Pizza's on its way, so get that cute little ass upstairs and get comfy."

She smiled then trudged up the stairs. By the time she came back down, the pizza had arrived and there was a plate and a glass of wine waiting on the coffee table for her. They spent the rest of the night cuddled on the couch, binge watching Hannah's favorite, Cobra Kai. She was so exhausted, she actually ended up in his bed for something other than hot sex.

Chapter Nineteen

"Good Morning, Beautiful," Mikael murmured in Hannah's ear.

"Mmm, hello Mr. Sexypants," she purred.

"Move in with me," Mikael blurted.

"Huh?" Hannah asked.

"I wanna wake up next to you every morning. Say yes."

"Yes," she exclaimed.

He pulled her close, crushed his lips to hers and jammed his tongue in her mouth. She moaned loudly as she intertwined her tongue with his. He rolled her onto her back, smiling as she opened her legs wide. He moved on top of her and swiftly thrust his dick as deep inside her as he could get, growling at how she felt wrapped around his erection. He felt her nails raking his back hard. She moved her hands down to his ass, alternating squeezes and smacks.

He moved off her, laid on his back and wagged his finger at her. She climbed on top of him, sliding her wet pussy down his cock. She rode him hard, her incredible breasts bouncing wildly. There was nothing he loved more than watching this incredible woman making love to him. And damn did she feel amazing. He heard her breathing and her moaning get louder as she neared release. She came hard, screaming as wave after wave of ecstasy rocked her body. The whole scene sent him over the edge and he emptied himself inside her. She collapsed next to him, both of them drenched in sweat. After a hot steamy shower together, they grabbed a quick breakfast then took Cocoa for a walk.

"I'm gonna head down to the shop and change over from Halloween to Thanksgiving. I'll be back in a while," Hannah announced.

"Okay, let's go," Mikael replied.

"You don't have to help."

"I know. I want to."

"You're so sweet."

"Am not," he said as he gave her a smack on her sexy ass.

Hannah and Mikael spent a couple of hours changing out all the decorations and doing a quick straightening of the shelves. When they were done, they went to Hannah's office to put everything away. Mikael sat down on the couch and pulled Hannah into his lap. Wrapping her in his arms, he kissed her hard, his hands slipping under her shirt. Just the feeling of his hands on her bare skin was all it took to turn on the faucet in her panties. She moaned into his mouth as she started wiggling in his lap.

"What are you trying to do me, woman?"

"Get your dick hard, duh," she joked.

"It worked."

"Mmmm."

Hannah climbed off his lap, and knelt in front of him. She unzipped his jeans, freeing his erection. Lowering her head, she wrapped her mouth around his dick, sucking hard as she ran her tongue up and down his shaft. She gently ran her fingers over his balls.

"So good," he groaned.

She stopped and stood up, then removed her jeans and panties. She sat down facing him and wrapped her pussy around him. She leaned in and kissed him passionately. He loved when she was assertive like this. They continued their intimate dance until their bodies took flight, climaxing together, two people who had become one together. Hannah collapsed against him, chest heaving as he held her close.

"I love you," she whispered.

"Love you too."

"I'm starving, wanna grab lunch?"

"I'd rather grab you."

"Later," she teased as she stood up and got dressed.

They locked up the shop and walked across the street to grab lunch at Garden of Eden. Eden greeted them warmly and took them to a cozy table in the corner. After they finished lunch, they drove to Hannah's house so she could pack some of her things. For today, she just grabbed about a week's worth of clothes and most of Cocoa's stuff. When they got to Mikael's house, he helped her carry everything inside.

"Welcome home, baby," he exclaimed.

"I'm so happy," she choked.

Mikael grabbed her hands, twirling her around the living room. Next thing they knew, they were both on their asses, laughing hysterically.

"I guess we spun a little too much," he laughed.

She was laughing so hard, she couldn't even answer. They just sat, gazing at each other, laughing so hard tears were pouring down their cheeks. A familiar voice snapped them out of their hysterics.

"Have you both flipped your lids?" they heard Dean ask.

Mikael stood then helped Hannah up.

"We were spinning around the living room and next thing you know, we both hit the floor," Mikael explained.

"We were celebrating my moving in," Hannah added.

Alex ran over and hugged her. "Congratulations, girl."

"Thank you," Hannah replied.

Dean shook Mikael's hand, smiling seeing his friend find the same happiness he found with Alex.

"We need to celebrate. How 'bout we hit the club tonight," Dean said.

"I'm in," Mikael said.

They looked at their women, who both nodded in agreement.

"Just don't let us get drunk this time, please," Hannah quipped.

"I second that," Alex added.

They all made plans to meet in the parking lot at 6. After Dean and Alex left, Mikael and Hannah went into the bedroom to start unpacking her clothes. After they were done, Mikael sat down on the bed, his eyes glued to Hannah.

"Baby, come sit with me on *our* bed," he directed.

She sat down next to her sexy man. Within seconds, his lips were on hers, his tongue exploring her mouth. She pulled away and stood in front of him. Grabbing her cell phone, she turned on one of her favorite sexy rock songs. She treated Mikael to an extremely naughty striptease, leaving him sitting on the bed with his mouth hanging open. He gawked as she ran her hands all over her own body. When he saw her teasing her own pussy, he could barely contain himself. He picked her naked body up in his arms and laid her down on the bed.

"Open those sexy legs," he commanded.

She spread her legs wide. Mikael knelt down and pulled her to the edge of the bed. He buried his face between her legs, and slid his tongue in her folds, running it up to her clit. She writhed beneath him as his tongue continued its assault on her swollen bud. He sucked her clit hard as he slid a couple fingers inside her.

"So good, suck harder," she moaned.

He sucked her harder while increasing the pressure of his fingers on her g-spot. She was writhing hard beneath him, her beautiful breasts bouncing hard as her entire body exploded into glorious convulsions of intense pleasure.

"Oh fuck, Mikael," she screamed.

He stood and took in her beauty, her sweat-soaked skin glistening in the bright afternoon sun that was streaming into their bedroom. He lowered himself onto her hot body and slid his dick inside her, thrusting hard. She wrapped her arms around him, pulling him close as he crushed his lips to hers. The feeling of moving his dick inside her beautiful body was incredible. His growls turned into a full-blown roar as he emptied a huge load of his warm cream inside her. He kissed her and laid down next to her.

Pulling her close, he whispered, "I love you, baby."

"Mmm, I love you," she purred.

After a quick nap, they showered and got ready to meet Dean and Alex at the club. Sunday night was Karaoke night, so Hannah was excited to get a chance to sing. Thanks to Mikael's love, she was feeling so much more comfortable with herself than before they got together. She was dressing in sexier outfits, which he loved. Tonight, she opted for jeans and a black lace camisole under a light v-neck sweater and black cowgirl boots. Mikael howled when he saw her.

They were pulling into the parking lot just as Dean and Alex were getting out of their truck, so the four of them walked inside together. Alex had already secured the table down front, a perk of knowing the owner. Mikael and Dean each ordered a beer, while the women opted for a glass of wine each, agreeing that would be their limit after the Halloween party shenanigans! Not long after they finished their drinks and meals, Doug walked onto the stage and announced the start of Karaoke. He spotted Hannah down front.

"Everyone, we have a fan-favorite with us tonight. Hannah, would you like to get us started?"

Hannah nodded yes, and grabbed Mikael's hand. He followed her onto the stage. Hannah found her favorite duet and started the song. She and Mikael crooned a beautiful version of the love song she picked out. Their performance was met with a standing ovation and a chant of encore. They picked out one more song, a more upbeat one this time, and delivered an equally amazing performance. After their second song, Hannah called Dean and Alex to follow them. The four of them did one last song as a group then headed back to their table to enjoy the rest of the aspiring singers.

Hannah and Alex excused themselves to freshen up. When they were out of earshot, Mikael said, "I wanna propose to Hannah."

"Hell yeah, man," Dean responded.

"I want you and Alex to be there."

"Got a plan in mind?"

"I want to propose on Christmas Day."

"I love that idea! Alex wants you two to come over for Christmas dinner. We would love to witness it, unless you want it to be private."

"I would love to have you both there."

"Count us in."

"Thanks, man."

Dean cleared his throat when he saw Alex and Hannah returning. They sat back down and watched the rest of the performances then they all headed out. They all decided to call it a night early, since Hannah and Alex had to work in the morning and Dean had classes. After everyone hugged goodnight, each couple headed home. Hannah was so excited that going home for her meant Mikael's house.

"What do you usually do for Thanksgiving?" Hannah asked.

"Usually pretending I loved Liza at her parents' house with dinner that contained not one traditional Thanksgiving food."

"I'm sorry, but I have some good news. I love preparing the traditional Thanksgiving meal."

"That makes me even happier than sex," he quipped.

Hannah laughed. "I was thinking of inviting Dean and Alex for dinner, if that's okay since it's your house."

"Our house, and of course it's okay."

"I promise, I'll get used to calling it that."

"Speaking of that, would you like me to pack more of your stuff while you're at work."

"Are you sure you don't mind?"

"Not at all. Just need to know what you want me to pack."

"I think clothes to start. The rest I'll have to decide on."

"Makes sense."

Mikael turned the opposite direction of his house. He pulled in at one of the scenic overlooks in their town. After exiting the truck, he walked around and opened Hannah's door then led her to the backseat. They climbed in and Mikael quickly pulled her close. He smashed his lips to hers and slid his tongue into her mouth. They sat in the backseat, making out like teenagers for close to an hour.

"I wanna fuck," Hannah announced.

Before Mikael could respond, Hannah wiggled out of her jeans and panties. She unzipped Mikael's pants and slid his hand inside his underwear, stroking his cock. He groaned, his dick hard as a rock, aching to feel her wrapped around him. She climbed onto his lap and took him into her. She angled herself so her clit rubbed his dick with every stroke. She bounced up and down, as they fucked hard and fast, both of them moaning loudly.

"Oh Mikael, you feel so good," she moaned.

"Ride me harder, Hannah," he commanded.

She fucked him even harder, feeling her body explode in ecstasy. Mikael quickly followed, shooting his load inside her. He pulled her close as they came down off their high, chests heaving, drenched in sweat. They headed home and after a quick shower, went to bed, quickly falling asleep.

The weeks leading up to Thanksgiving were busy. Between the shop and moving the rest of her stuff into Mikael's house, Hannah was exhausted. She decided to close the shop for the week before and week of the holiday. Kurt and Amanda were grateful for the break, even more so when Hannah told them she would still pay them. Dean had let them know that Andy and Lizzie would be flying in, so Hannah would be cooking for six instead of four. She was excited they would all be together, especially since when they first met, she never thought she would end up with Mikael.

Hannah had ordered her turkey since they tended to sell out as it got closer to the holiday. She went to the store the Saturday before to pick it up and purchase the rest of what she needed. Her menu, in addition to the turkey, included mashed potatoes, stuffing, green beans, and home-made gravy. She also stopped at the liquor store to stock up on wine and beer. After she dropped the groceries off, she ran over to her house to give it a quick cleaning, as Andy and Lizzie would be staying there during their visit.

When she was done, she headed back home and collapsed on the couch, quickly falling asleep. She woke up a couple hours later covered in a blanket. She smelled something delicious coming from the kitchen. When she wandered out there, she saw Mikael standing at the stove, finishing up a delicious looking dinner of spaghetti and meatballs.

"Hello there, sleepyhead," he teased.

"Sorry about that."

"No need, you've been working really hard."

"Can I help with anything?"

"No. I'm taking care of you tonight."

"You're amazing."

"Take a seat, dinner's almost ready."

Hannah sat at the table and waited. A few minutes later, Mikael carried two plates of food over. He grabbed a bottle of wine from the fridge and poured them each a glass. After clinking glasses, Hannah took a sip of wine then dug into her dinner.

"This is so delicious," she gushed.

Mikael smiled. "I'm glad you like it."

"Mmmm," she moaned, as she wolfed down her dinner.

After they were done, she tried to help cleanup, but he made her go sit on the couch. When he had finished, he joined her on the couch. Mikael wrapped an arm around her shoulders, and she laid her head on his shoulder. He grabbed the remote and found a movie for them to watch. It didn't take long before Hannah was softly snoring on his shoulder. He kissed the top of her head lightly, his heart bursting with love for his amazing woman. She awakened just as the movie was ending.

"Let's go to bed, baby."

"Sounds good," she yawned.

Mikael took Cocoa out for a last bathroom break then locked up the house. After turning all the lights out, he carried Hannah to the bathroom so she could get ready for bed. By the time Mikael had gotten ready and laid next to her, she was already sound asleep. He pulled the covers up, turned out the light and drifted off himself.

Chapter Twenty

They spent Sunday and Monday just relaxing. Tuesday morning, Hannah took the turkey out to thaw, then after breakfast, they drove to Philadelphia to pick Andy and Lizzie up from the airport. They waited in the cell phone lot until Andy called to let them know they were waiting out front. Hannah got out to help load their luggage into Mikael's truck. They had quite a bit as they were planning to stay through the New Year's holiday. Lizzie gave Hannah a big hug.

"I'm so happy to see Mikael with you instead of the she-devil," Lizzie whispered in Hannah's ear.

"I've never felt happier," Hannah whispered back.

Once they had everything loaded, Andy rode up front with Mikael, with Lizzie and Hannah in the backseat. They laughed all the way back to Lancaster, especially when Mikael told them the story about Hannah and Alex's drunken escapades on Halloween. When they got into town, they took Andy and Lizzie to Hannah's house to drop off their luggage then headed over to Dean and Alex's house. They made plans to get together the next night, as Andy and Lizzie were exhausted from traveling, so Mikael and Hannah drove them back to her house.

"We'll catch up tomorrow. We want to come see your shop," Lizzie said.

"Sounds good. Sleep well and let us know if you need anything," Hannah replied.

Mikael and Hannah headed home. After giving Cocoa her dinner and taking her for a quick walk, Hannah went into the kitchen to start getting some of the food ready for Thanksgiving. Mikael joined her and asked to be put to work.

"Thanks, but you don't need to do that."

"I want to."

"In that case, could you break up the bread for the stuffing?"

"I would rather stuff you, but for now, sure."

She gave him a light smack on the ass. "Naughty man."

"Because you're so damn hot!"

"Let me show how I want the size to be."

"The bread pieces, or my dick?"

"Mikael," she scolded.

"What?"

"Keep misbehaving and I send you to bed with no dinner."

"Okay, let's go to bed, baby."

She put her hands on her hips and gave him a look. He took one look at her face and got right to work. He watched her break up one piece of bread and did the rest the way she showed him. While he was doing that, she got the rest of the ingredients ready for the stuffing. That was all she wanted to get done tonight; the rest she would do on Wednesday. She put the stuffing in the fridge then asked Mikael what he wanted for dinner.

"You, of course."

Before she could say a word, she was over his shoulder, her head even with his ass.

"You better not fart," she joked.

"Hannah," he chided.

She was laughing so hard, she snorted. Mikael put her down and took her into his arms. His lips quickly found hers, his kiss soaking her panties. He quickly undressed her and laid her down in bed. He removed his own clothes and laid next to her, kissing her even more eagerly. He pulled her against him, his hand rubbing her ass, getting her even hotter. She started grinding against him, eager to feel him pleasure

155

her clit. She felt two fingers opening her folds and sliding inside her. He moved his fingers to her clit, rubbing softly at first then increasing his pressure.

"Oh Mikael, so good. Don't stop," she moaned.

He slid down her body and replaced his fingers with his tongue. He loved tasting his delicious woman. More than that, he loved the way she responded to his touch. Nothing was sexier to him than a woman who knew what she wanted in bed and wasn't afraid to ask for it. He licked and sucked her until she screamed out, rocking hard as ecstasy consumed her entire body.

"Get on your back. Now," she commanded.

Mikael laid on his back, smiling as he saw his sexy lover climb on top and lower her hot pussy on his cock. Fuck, he loved how it felt inside her, watching her hot tits bouncing hard as they fucked. She leaned back, bracing her hands on his muscular thighs. He rubbed her clit with his thumb as she rode him, matching her with his strong thrusts until they both exploded hard. They got cleaned up and dressed then ran out to grab some dinner.

They got back and spent the rest of the night camped out in front of the TV. Mikael wanted Hannah to get some rest, since she would be busy over the next couple days getting dinner ready. He was so excited for them to be able to host this dinner together, but he felt bad as he knew how much of a football fan she was and would be missing the game. That's when he came up with an idea. He couldn't wait to surprise her tomorrow. They ended up binge-watching one of their favorite shows until Hannah fell asleep on his shoulder. He carried her to bed, took Cocoa out for a potty break then locked everything up and joined her in their bed, falling asleep beside her.

The next morning, they went out to breakfast with Dean, Alex, Andy and Lizzie, then they all headed over to the pet shop so she could give Andy and Lizzie a tour.

"Make sure you show them your office," Mikael whispered.

That earned him an elbow in the side from Hannah. She walked Andy and Lizzie around the store while Mikael waited up front with Dean and Alex. She could hear them giggling a little.

"Okay, what's so funny?" Hannah asked.

"Alex may have told us what she overheard from the office one afternoon," Lizzie replied.

Looking at Andy, Hannah joked, "Your friend's a horndog."

They started laughing hysterically, their voices carrying in the quiet shop. Hannah took them to the infamous office, and told them how Mikael said if they ever made a movie, it would be called Pet Shop Passion. That led Andy to rename her office the Pet Shop Passion Pit. They headed back up front and were faced with three people standing there, hands on hips.

"Dare I ask what was so funny," Mikael said.

"A little birdie may have mentioned overhearing us in the office," Hannah said, nodding toward Alex.

"I hear you're a horndog," Andy added.

"Tell them what you renamed the office, babe," Lizzie said to Andy.

Andy told them the nickname, which had everyone laughing. After they were done with the tour, they all walked across the street to grab lunch at Eden's restaurant. Hannah had taken a liking to her and wanted to help her out. She had a feeling Eden was dealing with some pretty serious wounds from her past, but Hannah didn't know her well enough to ask. Hannah stuck with offering her support by patronizing her restaurant and having fliers on the counter at her store.

"Anyone up for a club outing tonight?" Dean asked.

Alex, Andy and Lizzie all said yes. Mikael looked at Hannah.

"Up to you, baby, since you have food to make," Mikael said.

"Most of what I have left needs to wait until morning, so count me in."

Mikael and Hannah headed back home. She wanted to get the pies made today so all she had to do tomorrow was the actual food. Mikael made a quick stop at an electronics store on the way home, but wouldn't let her come in. She wondered what he was up to. He came out a little while later, but wouldn't show her what he bought. When they got back to the house, Mikael told her to wait in the bedroom until he called her.

"Okay, you can come out," he yelled after a little while.

Hannah walked into the kitchen and saw that he had setup a small flat screen TV on the counter.

"I wanted you to be able to see the games while you were cooking tomorrow," he said.

"Thank you. I truly don't deserve you."

Pulling her close, he responded, "We deserve each other. I love you."

"I love you too."

"Put me to work. Let's get those pies done."

After the pies were done baking, they put them out of Cocoa's reach to cool. They showered together then got dressed. Mikael took one look at his sexy woman and his jaw dropped. She was wearing tight black jeans and a yellow low-cut t-shirt. He remembered back to one of their early meetings and how much he loved her in yellow.

"It's gonna be a miracle if we make it to the club," he flattered.

"I guess you like what you see," she cooed.

He kissed her hard, his desire spilling over. He wanted her so damn bad, but it would have to wait unless they wanted to stand up their friends. They finished getting ready and drove to the club. They were first to arrive, so they found an empty table and sat down. Hannah texted Alex and Lizzie to let them know. The rest of the group arrived a little while later. When one of their favorite sexy rock songs came on, Hannah, Alex, and Lizzie hit the dance floor.

"Damn, we have the three hottest babes in here," Mikael declared.

Dean and Andy agreed as they sat there watching their women, shit-eating grins on their faces. After a couple of hours of dancing, Hannah was starting to feel tired. She asked Mikael if they could head out since she needed to be up early in the morning to start cooking. They hugged everyone goodnight then walked out to Mikael's truck. Once they got inside, Hannah took Cocoa outside for a last potty break, then locked up.

"I need to make sure I'm up by 7 tomorrow morning or dinner will be late."

"I'll set the alarm on my phone."

"Thanks."

They headed straight to bed and both quickly fell asleep. The next morning, Mikael woke up a little before seven. Hannah was still asleep, so Mikael watched her for a few minutes before he woke her up.

"Good Morning, beautiful," Mikael whispered.

"Good Morning, handsome," Hannah cooed.

"What do you want for breakfast?" he asked.

"A nice big piece of weenie-toast," she joked.

"Hannah!"

"What?"

"Naughty girl."

"I can't help you have such a yummy cock."

"Woman!"

Hannah smiled as she got out of bed and got ready to shower. She put a little wiggle in her ass for Mikael's benefit. She heard him come up behind her and join her. After a hot, steamy shower together, they went to the kitchen for a quick breakfast. After they finished, Hannah got the turkey ready and into the oven. She had a little bit of time before she had to do some more cooking, so she took Cocoa for a walk. When she got back, she saw the dining room table was all set.

"Thank you," she said.

"Anything else I can do?"

"You don't have to help."

"I know. I want to."

"Okay. I want to get the cole slaw ready next."

Mikael helped her with that then helped her peel and dice the potatoes. She was also making creamed spinach, green bean casserole, and candied yams. He couldn't believe how much food they had, and even more so, that this amazing woman was preparing everything. He still sometimes shook his head in disbelief at how he let Liza treat him. Hannah couldn't have been more opposite of the she-devil. He walked over and pulled her close, kissing her tenderly.

"What was that for?"

"For being you. I love you."

"I love you so much."

Once they had everything they needed prepped, they took a much-needed rest on the porch. They were sitting on the steps kissing when Dean and Alex, along with their dog Holly, got there. Dean honked his horn when he saw them. Not breaking the kiss, Mikael gave him the finger. Andy and Lizzie pulled in a few minutes later. Mikael and

Hannah finally came up for air and stood to greet their friends, all standing there looking amused.

"I'd tell you two to get a room, but you'd probably do it," Dean joked.

That earned him another finger from Mikael, as everyone laughed. He wanted today to be a great day. Hannah deserved that with all the work she put into this meal. They all walked inside, and Holly immediately went over and laid with Cocoa. Mikael put football on the living room TV then came in and did the same on the kitchen TV so Hannah could watch. Everyone else sat down in the living room while Hannah worked on the meal. A few minutes later, Lizzie and Alex walked into the kitchen to see if she needed any help.

"Thanks, but I'm good." Hannah said.

She was just about done with all the food, so she started to put everything into serving dishes. Alex and Lizzie started carrying things to the table for her. Once the rest of the food was on the table, Hannah took the turkey out. She got the stuffing out and into a dish then put the turkey onto her serving platter and carried it to the table. She heard both dogs start panting and laughed. Mikael called everyone to the table. He walked to the head of the table where Hannah had placed the bird. Before he started carving, he addressed the group.

"Thanks everyone for coming here to celebrate today. I truly consider all of you family. My biggest thanks, though, go to the beautiful, sexy, amazing woman at the other end of the table. Baby, everything looks delicious and I can't wait to get a taste," he said with a wink.

After he carved the turkey, he passed the tray around the table. Once everyone had turkey, the rest of the dishes were passed until nobody had room left on their plates. Not one person left any food on their plate, all of them agreeing how amazing a cook Hannah was. Once everyone was done, the guys retired to the living room, all them in food comas. Hannah started clearing the table but Alex and Lizzie stopped her.

"Girl, you did enough. Let us clean up," Alex said.

"I'm with Alex. Go take seat on that sexy man of yours' lap." Lizzie added.

"Thank you, ladies," Hannah yawned.

She walked into the living room, but there were no open seats, so she stood behind Mikael. After a few minutes, she yawned loudly. Mikael got up and motioned for her to take his seat next to Dean. She plopped down on the couch, her eyes drooping. Mikael stood behind her, massaging her shoulders. He kissed her to the top of her head and thanked her again for making such a wonderful meal. It wasn't long before she fell asleep on Dean's shoulder. He motioned for Mikael, who lifted her off the couch and carried her to their bed. The other ladies had finished cleaning up by then and had rejoined their men.

"Why don't we head out so Hannah can sleep," Alex suggested to the group.

Everyone agreed and thanked Mikael for having them. They all also asked him to thank Hannah again for the amazing meal. Mikael walked outside with them so he could let Cocoa out. Once everyone was gone, he locked up, turned out the lights and joined Hannah in the bedroom. He undressed her and got her into her sleepwear, then got himself ready for bed. He pulled the covers up, turned off the light and quickly fell asleep himself.

Chapter Twenty-One

Thanksgiving was only the start of the busy holiday season, both for her shop and personally. After seeing how exhausted she was after Thanksgiving, Mikael decided he was going to take Hannah away for Christmas. He knew she would be closing the shop after the weekend before Christmas to give her employees extra time with their families. One of the things he loved most about her was how she put everyone else's needs ahead of her own, so he made sure he took care of her needs. Once Hannah left for work, he made the arrangements for their trip. Now he only had to figure out what to get her for Christmas.

Hannah opened the store a little early Monday morning so she could take down all the Thanksgiving decorations and replace them with winter ones. Once Kurt arrived, he helped her and they had the store decorated before any customers arrived. This was an especially busy time for her as people tended to holiday shop for their pets, as well as the pet lovers in their life. She always kept extra stock on hand, especially of her most popular items. Things were so busy today, they didn't have time to stop for lunch. Of course, that wasn't an issue when she had such a thoughtful boyfriend.

A little before noon, she looked up when the door opened and saw Mikael carrying a bag of food. As soon as they had a little lull, he started unpacking the bags. He had opted for Chinese food, which smelled delicious. They all sat and enjoyed lunch together, Hannah waiting on customers as they came in, so Kurt could take a lunch break. It never stopped amazing Mikael how she cared for her employees.

"I feel bad that Amanda never gets to join us," Hannah lamented.

"I know, so that's why I dropped her off some lunch first then came here," Mikael responded.

"You're the best."

"I know and that's why I have another surprise for you."

"Ooh, I love surprises, especially from you."

"I want to take you away for Christmas. You worked so hard on Thanksgiving that I want you to relax for Christmas."

"Oh, Mikael, that sounds great."

"Awesome, I booked a beautiful cabin this morning. I have a feeling we'll quickly end up on Santa's naughty list."

"You bet we will!"

"Are you up for a small gathering tonight?" Mikael asked.

"Depends on what," she responded.

"Dean called and wants to have us, and Andy and Lizzie over for dinner and maybe a game."

"That sounds like fun."

"Great, I'll text him quick and let him know, as I wanted to check with you first."

"Thank you so much."

Before he could say anything else, traffic started to increase in the store, so she had to focus on that. Mikael took care of cleaning up from their lunch. As soon as she had a quick minute, he let her know he was heading out so she could focus on her customers. He stopped by Dean's on the way home, so he could let them know they would be over tonight and to talk to Alex about ideas for a Christmas gift for Hannah.

"That's a toughie. She's always been one to prefer giving rather than receiving. I can tell you this much, she will appreciate sentiment over price any day," Alex said.

"That gives me an idea. Thank you," Mikael responded.

"Now you have me curious."

"Andy sent me a couple pictures he took of us dancing at your different wedding gatherings, so I'm going to get a frame that will hold them, along with a poem I wrote about her after the first time I saw her."

"She will love that!"

Mikael thanked her for the help, told them they'd be over later and headed home to wait for Hannah. He had a little something fun for her in mind before they went to Dean's later. When he got home, he did a few things around the house, then went into their bedroom. He knew about what time she got home, so he wanted to make sure he was ready. He had a feeling she was going to love his latest surprise.

Hannah was stressed by the time she finished work, as they were busier than they had been in a while. She needed something to calm her a bit before they went out tonight, figuring a glass of wine would do the trick. When she got inside, Mikael wasn't waiting in the living room like usual. She looked down and noticed a trail of rose petals leading to their bedroom, so she started following the trail. A huge smile crept onto her face when she saw what was waiting for her.

Mikael was standing next to the bed wearing only a bow tie and holding a red rose in his hand. Her eyes immediately lowered, unable to miss what was sticking out from his body. Not saying a word, he handed her the rose and quickly started tearing her clothes off. He scooped her up and laid her down on the bed. He crushed his lips to hers, his tongue eagerly exploring every inch of her mouth. He quickly slid down her body and jammed his tongue into her pussy, licking her clit hard.

She lifted her hips off the bed, moaning at the intensity with which he pleasured her clit. He slid a couple fingers into her folds, stroking her g-spot hard. Her entire body was on fire, bucking with the incredible pleasure she was experiencing. It didn't take long before she shattered and her entire body convulsed with a powerful climax that left her screaming. Mikael moved on top of her, his dick easily sliding into her pussy, soaking wet from her orgasm. He fucked her hard and fast, both of them panting and groaning as he emptied his load deep inside her. He moved next to her, as they both laid there drenched in sweat, chests heaving, bodies tingling from their incredible fuck.

"Damn, you aways know what I need," Hannah panted.

"You're so fuckin' hot," Mikael declared.

Once they could breathe again, they showered together and got ready to head over to Dean and Alex's. When they got there and went inside, Cocoa beelined for Holly and the two pups started playing. Leo laid down next to them and quickly fell asleep. Alex walked over to Hannah.

"I know what you did before you came over. I can see it on your face," Alex teased.

"I didn't get anything on my face," Hannah protested.

"Oh my god, I just meant you had a huge smile on your face."

Hannah blushed. "Oh, duh. See what that man does to me?"

They both laughed out loud, earning them curious looks from Mikael and Dean. Andy and Lizzie arrived a few minutes later. They walked in and saw Hannah and Alex still laughing hysterically. Andy shook his head and joined the other guys while Alex filled Lizzie in, causing her to snort from laughing so hard. Three loud throat clears snapped them out of their hysterics and they joined the guys in the living room. Alex grabbed a tray of burgers from the fridge and handed them to Dean, who went outside to the grill to start cooking, Mikael and Andy in tow. Lizzie and Hannah helped Alex put the rest of the food out. Alex poured them each a glass of wine and they sat around the kitchen table sharing dirty stories about their men.

Once the burgers were done, the guys came back in and everyone sat down to eat. The guys desperately tried to find out what the ladies were laughing about but they wouldn't budge. They even tried pretending to pout, but to no avail. After they cleaned up from dinner, they moved into the living room for a men vs. women game of Charades. Of course, the women won the game, a whopping 20-0.

"Too bad we weren't playing strip Charades. We could've compared notes," Hannah quipped.

"You're in trouble later for that, babe," Mikael chastised.

"Oh, I'm shaking now," Hannah mocked.

"You will be when my dick gets done with you," Mikael warned.

Andy, Lizzie, Dean, and Alex stood there, mouths hanging open.

"Mikael, what have you done to my friend?" Alex inquired.

"Unleashed her inner dirty girl," Mikael declared.

Everyone laughed as Hannah's face turned bright red.

"Damn kitty litter," Hannah joked.

"I'm not sure I want to know," Andy said.

Mikael and Hannah smiled, neither willing to give up the circumstances that led to their first sexual encounter. Hannah had a feeling Alex wasn't going to stop until she got her to spill, but for tonight, they all let it go. Once they had finished the game and cleaned up, Hannah was getting antsy to get home and see what Mikael had in store for her!

"How about tomorrow night, we split up? Girls night for us and guys night for them," Lizzie asked.

Everyone agreed and firmed up plans. Hannah and Mikael got in his car and started towards home. Her panties were soaked with anticipation of what her punishment would be for her dirty comments. She wanted him so damn bad, she could practically taste him, and fuck if he wasn't delicious! They pulled into the driveway, and Hannah was so eager she couldn't wait until they got inside, instead climbing into the back of his truck. He joined her and she quickly had him out of his pants. After removing her own pants and climbed on top of him.

Mikael growled as he felt her warm wetness wrap around him. Fuck, this woman was insatiable and damn did she feel good. He held her waist as she bounced her sexy body up and down his cock, angling herself for maximum friction. She moaned loudly as everything was being stimulated and driving her wild. Mikael's strong hands moved to her ass, squeezing hard, driving her even more wild. She rode hard and fast until wave after wave of pleasure consumed her from head to toe. Mikael quickly followed, emptying himself into her.

"Holy shit, woman!"

"I hope the neighbors didn't hear that."

"Fuck it, they're assholes anyway."

"Then I'll scream louder next time."

He kissed her hard as they got dressed and went inside to head to bed. The next day was no less busy at the shop and Hannah was exhausted, but she was looking forward to a night out with Lizzie and Alex. Alex picked Lizzie up first then picked her up at Mikael's house. They decided to start with a quick bite to eat then Christmas shopping for their men. The first stop they made was an "adult" store. They all decided on naughty Santa outfits guaranteed to land them on Santa's naughty list. They decided to hit the music shop next to see if they could find something special. After quite a bit of time and some assistance from the staff, they couldn't wait to surprise the guys. After their shopping excursion, they went to Eden's restaurant to relax before heading home.

"All right, girl, spill it," Alex prodded Hannah.

"Spill what?" Hannah asked.

"You know what. Kitty litter. Tell us now," Alex exclaimed.

"Mikael was trying to get me to come to his house, but at that point, I hadn't regained my confidence and I wouldn't let myself get involved. So one evening, he called the shop and told me he was out of kitty litter and asked me to bring some by. Let's just say I ended up waking up there the next morning."

Hannah's confession was met with a couple low whistles. The three of them burst out laughing. Hannah quickly got lost, thinking about that night with Mikael. He made her feel incredible and even more importantly, made her fee like she was beautiful and desirable. Alex's voice snapped her out of her reverie.

"Eden's waiting to take your order."

"I'm sorry, I would like a BLT and an iced tea," Hannah said.

Eden smiled and headed to the kitchen to put their order in. Lizzie and Alex were sitting there looking amused.

"Where were you?" Lizzie asked.

"Daydreaming about kitty litter," Hannah joked.

After they finished eating, they headed to Alex's car. She dropped Lizzie at Hannah's house then drove to Mikael's to take Hannah home. Hannah was still getting used to thinking of Mikael's house as her home. She loved him so much and she couldn't be happier. The guys weren't home yet, so Alex came in. A few minutes later, Alex's phone rang.

"Okay, we'll be right there," Hannah heard Alex tell whoever called. "The guys had a bit too much to drink. That was Doug. He took their keys so we need to go get them." Alex explained.

"There's more room in my car, so I'll drive," Hannah said.

They drove down to the club and parked in front of the door. They walked inside and saw three men with goofy grins on their faces.

Hannah and Alex walked over, pretending to be annoyed. They helped Dean and Mikael out to the car then came back for Andy. Once Andy and Mikael were in Hannah's car, she helped Alex get Dean into his truck. She told Hannah she would be over tomorrow to get her car. Hannah waved and headed to her house to drop Andy off. She called Lizzie to let her know what happened.

Lizzie was waiting outside when Hannah pulled up, so she walked over to help get Andy inside. Once they got him settled, she hugged Lizzie goodbye and took Mikael home. She got him into the bedroom and laid him down. She removed his clothes down to his underwear and got him tucked in bed. He quickly passed out, so Hannah watched a little TV before heading to bed herself. She called Alex and Lizzie the next day and found out that Dean and Andy were suffering as bad as Mikael. Hannah was in the kitchen cooking breakfast when he shuffled in, looking like death.

"Good morning, Sunshine," Hannah yelled.

"I deserved that," Mikael lamented.

"Yep. Breakfast is ready."

After Mikael ate, he went back to bed, while Hannah cleaned up and went to work. The rest of the time leading up to their getaway went quickly. She closed the shop for the final time until after New Year's Day then headed home to finish packing. Mikael still hadn't told her where he was taking her, but she knew no matter the location, they would have fun. They stopped by Dean and Alex's to drop Cocoa and Leo off, then got on the road.

"Are you going to tell me where we're going?" Hannah asked.

"If you pay attention, you'll figure it out," Mikael teased.

Hannah stuck her tongue out and folded her arms across her chest before bursting out in laughter. Mikael shook his head, before laughing along with her. After a little while of driving, she started seeing signs that let her know where they were going and she couldn't contain her excitement.

"Are you really taking me to Hershey?" she asked.

"Yes."

"Yay! I've always wanted to see the light display they put up."

"If we ever make it out of the cabin."

"Oooh, naughty man!"

They arrived about an hour later. The cabin Mikael rented was stunning. The first floor had a kitchen and dining area and a large living room with a fireplace. The second floor had the bedroom and a large bathroom that included a walk-in shower and a heart-shaped soaking tub for two. Lots of places for naked fun, she thought to herself. She noticed a basket on the counter in the kitchen and was delighted to see it filled with samples of different Hershey chocolate bars. What she really hoped for, though, was a sample of Hershey's chocolate syrup! She opened the cabinets in the kitchen and felt her heart start racing when she saw a bottle. All the rooms were decorated for Christmas and it was truly breathtaking.

Mikael walked into the kitchen after taking their luggage up to the bedroom and saw her holding the syrup. He took one look at the wicked smile on her face and knew what she was thinking. He walked over and pulled her in close, kissing her hard. She melted into him, her tongue exploring every corner of his sexy mouth. Mikael stopped kissing her when he heard her stomach growl.

"Let's go grab some dinner," he suggested.

"Sounds good."

They drove to a small diner they had passed on their way to the cabin. Once they finished eating, Mikael drove to a nearby farm and parked. He took her inside and told them he had a reservation. Hannah had no idea for what, but she was excited. The owner took them outside where she saw a sleigh hooked up to a small tractor. Mikael helped her climb inside then sat down next to her, wrapping them in the blanket that was provided. They were then treated to an hour-long tour of the farm, beautifully decorated with holiday lights. The setting was one of the most romantic things she'd ever seen. Mikael wrapped an arm around her shoulders and she laid her head on his shoulder. She looked over at him, closing her eyes as he leaned in for a kiss.

Once the ride was over, they drove back to the cabin. Mikael built a fire in the fireplace and poured them each a glass of wine. They sat on the rug in front of the fire and drank their wine. Once they had both finished, Mikael laid her down and wrapped his arms around her, kissing her tenderly on her beautiful mouth. Their tongues danced together, exploring each other's mouths. Mikael slid his hands under her shirt, setting her skin on fire. He removed her shirt and bra and started showering her breasts with kisses. He gently flicked each nipple with his tongue.

He removed her socks and shoes, then off came the rest of her clothes. She loved the feeling of the fire on her naked skin, but even more, she loved the feeling of Mikael's hands and mouth on her. She reached up and removed his shirt, exposing his sexy chest. She removed this rest of his clothes, her eyes drinking in his sexiness. She spread her legs wide, letting him know exactly what she wanted. He put his head between her legs and gave her pussy one hell of a tongue lashing. She could feel her orgasm building, and just as she was about to explode, Mikael stopped licking her.

He moved on top of her, sliding his hands under her ass and sliding his dick inside her. She was so sensitive from almost exploding that every thrust from her sexy lover drove her wild. Her body started quaking until she lost all control and screamed as she rode huge waves of incredible ecstasy. The feeling of her constricting around him was more than he could take and he filled her with his hot lava.

When they were done, Hannah stretched and let out a big yawn. Mikael grabbed a blanket and a couple pillows off the couch, placing one of the pillows under her beautiful head. He extinguished the fire and laid down next to her, covering them with the blanket. They quickly fell asleep, still naked and holding each other close.

Chapter Twenty-Two

Hannah awakened the next morning, Christmas Eve, and couldn't believe her eyes. She was by herself still on the floor and there was now a big Christmas tree in the corner of the living room. Mikael was sitting at the dining table, fully dressed in tight jeans and a flannel shirt, the sexiest damn lumberjack she'd ever laid eyes on.

"This is amazing," Hannah gushed. "I can't believe I slept through this."

"Must have been that hot sex, you were out cold," he teased. "Nothing but the best for my woman. I also brought decorations with me, so we can trim it later."

"I'm so excited."

"I can't think of anyone I'd rather spend the holidays with than you, baby. I love you."

"I love you too."

He pulled her in close and asked, "What would you like for breakfast?"

"Your sausage, please."

"What am I going to do with you, woman?"

"I can think of some things. Seriously, though, how about we go back to the diner?"

"Sounds good."

They both splurged at the diner and ordered Belgian waffles covered in chocolate syrup and whipped cream. Hannah kept shifting her eyes between the waffle and her sexy man, her mouth looking like the Cheshire cat. Mikael could only imagine what was going on inside that dirty brain of hers.

"Okay, spill it woman."

"Just picturing eating this off your body."

"My naughty woman."

"You brought her out of hiding."

He smiled as he took a forkful of whipped cream and slowly licked it. That was all it took and Hannah felt a wetness between her legs. Not to be outdone, she repeated his move while flashing her best "bedroom eyes." She smiled when she saw his mouth drop open. Suddenly, she couldn't wait to get back to the cabin. They both finished their breakfast at record speed and raced back.

They barely had the door shut before clothes were flying everywhere. Hannah walked over to the couch and knelt backwards, giving Mikael a nice view of her bottom. He walked over and stood behind her, hands on her waist. She moaned as she felt his dick plunge into her pussy. He reached one hand around and teased her clit while pounding her with powerful thrusts, as they groaned with pleasure. They both quickly exploded, chests heaving, bodies drenched in sweat.

"How about we take a soak in the tub?" he asked breathlessly.

"Mmmm, sounds like heaven."

Hannah grabbed the bottle of chocolate syrup then they walked upstairs and into the bathroom. Mikael started the tub and put some bubbles in, while Hannah put the bottle of syrup in the bedroom. He helped Hannah into the tub then joined her. Once the tub was full, he turned off the water, and folded up two towels. They both leaned back and closed their eyes, enjoying the warm water and vanilla scented bubbles. She felt Mikael's hand start rubbing her back, which felt amazing. She loved their hard, fast fucking, but she also equally loved his more tender touching, sexual or not. She let out a contented sigh, loving the feeling of being with him. When they were done, they drained the tub then got in the shower to rinse off, then got dressed and went downstairs.

"Can we decorate the tree now?" Hannah asked, bouncing up and down.

"Yes, silly girl," Mikael laughed.

Mikael grabbed the suitcase that had the decorations and opened it on the dining table. Hannah couldn't believe her eyes. In one of their many chats before they got together, she told him who some of her favorite characters were and he remembered all of them. There were ornaments featuring Sesame Street, Looney Tunes, Winnie the Pooh, and Peanuts, just to name a few. She felt her eyes start leaking, so she walked over and wrapped her arms around him.

"Thank you," she whispered.

He took his thumb and wiped away her tears, kissing her tenderly. He had never before felt so much love for another person.

"I have been buying these as I came across them. I would love for this to become one of our holiday traditions."

"Oh, Mikael," she cooed.

They took turns taking ornaments over until the entire tree was decorated. Mikael handed her a box of tinsel, grinning as he watched her dance around the tree sprinkling tinsel on all the branches. She reminded him of a fairy spreading her magic dust. The childlike joy on her face melted his heart. The big, bad rock star turned into a puddle of goo whenever this woman was around. When she was done, he grabbed her and started twirling her around the living room.

"I have a couple of surprises for you tonight, and before you ask, you'll find out," he announced.

"Ooh, I can't wait," she exclaimed.

As dusk was just setting in, they headed out to a local pizza place for dinner. After they ate, Mikael headed for Hershey Park for their Christmas light display. The display was stunning and Hannah loved being able to see it with Mikael. They held hands the entire time, oblivious to any other people being around. After they had seen everything, they headed back to the cabin and went upstairs. Mikael sat down on the bed while Hannah grabbed a bag out of her suitcase.

"I have a surprise for you. Wait right here," she directed.

She walked out a few minutes later and Mikael's chin hit the floor. Before him stood his beautiful woman. She was wearing a red halter dress that showed plenty of cleavage, with a white bow and white fur around the bottom, along with red gloves. She finished off the outfit with red heels trimmed with white fur. She sauntered over to him, as his dick threatened to rip right through his pants.

"Holy shit, baby. You're stunning."

She smiled and slowly bent over in front him, and much to his delight, she was going commando. She got on the bed and crawled over to him.

"I'm here to make all your wishes come true," she breathed.

Mikael was unable to form words and instead just stared at her, tongue hanging out of his mouth. She lifted his shirt off and tossed it to the floor. He shivered as her soft gloved hands explored his sexy chest. She pushed him on his back and opened his jeans, freeing his erection. She removed his boots and socks then slid his pants down and tossed them with his shirt.

She grabbed the bottle of chocolate syrup and squeezed some onto his chest. She ran her tongue all over his chest until every last bit of chocolate was gone.

"Mmm, that was delicious, and the chocolate was pretty good too. Now, tell me what you desire," she said with a sultriness that drove him crazy.

"There is one thing I've been thinking about since the first time we did it," he confessed.

"Tell me, Mr. Sexy."

"I wanna taste that sweet pussy while those pouty lips are wrapped around my dick."

"Mmmm, Mikael," she purred.

She removed her dress and was about to remove her shoes when Mikael stopped her.

"Please, baby, leave them on," he begged.

She smiled and straddled him so his head was between her legs. She lowered her head and swallowed every inch of his delicious cock. She gasped as she felt his tongue enter her folds and tease her clit. He slid a couple fingers inside her, stroking her g-spot hard. Her entire body was bucking as she slid her lips and tongue up and down his perfect cock. Her entire body started quaking as she moved closer and closer to coming undone. When Mikael started sucking on her clit, that was all it took and she exploded all over his face. She moaned loudly as she sucked him harder and faster until she felt her mouth fill with his warm cream, which she quickly swallowed. She licked until she had every bit of his cum cleaned up. The feel of her lips had him hard again.

"On your back, now, baby," he commanded.

She did as she was told, spreading her legs wide. He loved the view of that sweet pussy, and quickly slid inside her pussy, still so slick and wet from her orgasm. He slowly and deliberately slid in and out of her, holding her tight. The intimacy when they made love like this was unmatched. She gazed into those beautiful sapphires and wrapped her arms and legs around him. The feeling of the faux fur on her shoes was tickling him as he continued his tender thrusts. He leaned down and kissed her hard as he filled another part of her with his cream. When he was done, he removed her shoes and tossed them on the floor then laid down next to her and pulled her in close.

"I think it's safe to say that put us at the top of Santa's naughty list," he teased.

"It was one hell of a ride," she declared.

Mikael pulled the covers up and turned off the lights. They fell asleep still holding each other, neither stirring until well after the sun's rays filled the room. Mikael woke up and stretched, jarring Hannah from her slumber. She rolled over so she was facing him. He pulled her close and kissed her tenderly.

"Merry Christmas, beautiful," he whispered.

"Merry Christmas, sexy," she squealed.

"I think Santa left something for you," he smiled.

"I believe he left something for you too," she replied.

They each walked to their suitcase and got a present out. Hannah handed hers to Mikael and he did the same. Mikael opened his first and couldn't believe what he saw. Hannah had found sealed original vinyl copies of every record Mikael's former band released.

"Hannah, this is amazing. How did you do this?"

"I found some at a vintage record store and Dean made some calls and helped me find the rest."

"Thank you."

"My pleasure."

"It will be later. Now, open yours!"

Hannah unwrapped her gift and tears immediately spilled out of her eyes. She just sat there, holding her gift, unable to say a word. She looked at Mikael, tears streaming down her cheeks. He gave her a large frame that included pictures of them dancing at Dean and Alex's bachelor/bachelorette party, rehearsal dinner, and wedding. The frame also had a short poem Mikael wrote shortly after they met.

Eyes the color of trees
Her yellow dress brings me to my knees
Sun-kissed skin topped with hair of cocoa
The mere sight of her activates my libido
Her body so divine
I want to make her mine

Finally able to speak, she gushed, "This is the most incredible and thoughtful gift anyone's ever given me."

"I know the poem isn't great, but that's why I never write lyrics."

"Actually, I think it's the best poem I've ever read."

They embraced, as Mikael kissed her tenderly. They showered, dressed then headed downstairs to make breakfast. Once they were done and packed, they were driving back as Dean and Alex were having the group over for Christmas dinner. Mikael carried all the luggage downstairs. He was always such a gentleman, well, except in the bedroom!

"What about the ornaments?" Hannah asked.

"We can leave them for now."

"What if someone else rents the cabin?"

"Oh, yeah, I forgot, I have one more Christmas present for you."

"What?"

"I bought the cabin. It's ours to use whenever we want a getaway."

"You never stop surprising me, my sexy man."

"And I never will. I love you."

"I love you too."

After they finished cleaning up and loading Mikael's truck, they got on the road. Hannah, being the unfailingly generous woman she always was, was trying to figure out what she would have time to make to bring to Dean and Alex's house. She didn't like going to anyone's home without a gift.

"I knew that's exactly what you were going to say, babe, so I took care of it," Mikael informed her.

"You think of everything. What did you get?"

"Two bottles of wine and an engraved Christmas ornament with their wedding date on it."

"Thank you so much. I also have something for Holly from my shop, so we're all set."

When they got home, they showered and dressed. For fun, Dean and Alex asked everyone to dress up for dinner. Mikael wore a tux and damn did he look stunning. Hannah surprised Mikael with the dress she bought, a floor length satin dress in his favorite yellow. If only she knew the real reason they were dressed up. Everything he needed for his plan was safely tucked away at Dean and Alex's house. He put his arm out and Hannah linked hers through it, as they walked out to his truck. He helped Hannah in, then walked around to the driver's seat. He was quiet on the ride over, as his nerves started getting the better of him. He was especially nervous by the time they arrived, and hoped Hannah didn't notice.

Everyone else was already there and looking gorgeous. Hannah handed Alex the wine and the gift they brought. She handed Holly's gift to Alex as well. Alex handed it to Holly, who opened it herself. Lizzie and Hannah went into the kitchen to help Alex get all the food into serving dishes, giving Dean a chance to sneak a couple things to Mikael. They already had a plan for his final surprise of the day for his precious Hannah. Mikael put the small velvet box in his pocket and hid the yellow roses on his chair. Once all the food was on the table, Dean put a glass of champagne at every seat. The men each pulled their woman's chair out, themselves remaining standing.

"Thank you all for joining us tonight," Dean said. "Mikael asked me if he could do a toast before dinner. Take it away, man."

"Thanks Dean. This year has been quite a roller coaster for me. I was about as low as a person could feel until an amazing woman changed everything. Hannah, my love, you are the kindest, sweetest, sexiest, naughtiest woman I've ever known and I love you more than anything. I never want to spend another night without you in my arms."

Before he continued, Mikael dropped to one knee. Dean handed him the bouquet, which he handed to Hannah. Mikael then pulled the ring box out of his pocket and opened it.

"Hannah Alice Davidson, will you do me the honor of becoming my wife?"

With tears streaming down her beautiful face, Hannah exclaimed, "Yes! Oh. Mikael, I love you."

Mikael placed the ring on her finger, then stood up. Hannah jumped out of her chair and threw her arms around Mikael, kissing him hard, as the rest of the group applauded. Not to be left out, Holly and Cocoa barked their approval, earning them a round of laughter. After a group hug, everyone stood behind their chair as Dean grabbed his glass of champagne.

"A toast to my beautiful wife for preparing a delicious meal. I'd also like to toast spending the holiday with friends who are also family. And finally, a toast to Mikael and Hannah. Now, let's eat!"

Everyone clinked glasses and took a sip of champagne then sat down. Everyone ate way more than they should have, but Alex was just as amazing a cook as Hannah. Not surprisingly, once everything was cleaned up, Mikael and Hannah took an early exit, eager to get home and celebrate in their favorite way. They raced home and quickly went inside. After giving Cocoa and Leo their presents and laughing as Cocoa opened hers while Leo just sauntered away from his, they headed to their bedroom. Mikael unzipped her dress and removed it, hanging it over the chair. He just stood there staring at his fiancee in her matching yellow bra and panties and yellow heels.

"You truly are a vision in yellow," he cooed. "But now, I want to see nothing but skin."

Hannah licked her lips as she removed her bra, running her hands over her breasts. She slid her panties off then kicked off her shoes. She walked over to Mikael and quickly got him out of his tux. He pulled her close, skin on skin, and kissed her hard, loving the feel of her body heat. He scooped her up and carried her over to the bed, and gently laid her down. He joined her and pulled her in tight.

"Baby, you made me the happiest man in the world tonight. I hope you have plenty of energy; you're going to need it!"

"Oh, Mikael" was all she managed to utter before his lips crashed into hers, tongue exploring every inch of her mouth as she twirled hers with his. He lifted her arms above her head then ran his hands down the sides of her body, filling her skin with goosebumps. Gently spreading her legs, his hands and lips explored the insides of her thighs, inching ever so close to the place she wanted him most. Sucking the insides of her thighs had her bucking beneath him, desperately trying to get his tongue on her pussy.

"Please, I need to feel your tongue on my clit," she moaned.

He slipped his tongue between her folds, slowly and deliberately running his tongue up to her clit, lightly teasing her. Her breathing quickened as she moaned at his touch. He continued applying light pressure, driving her wild. She was aching for the assault he usually unleashed on her.

"Please, baby, suck my clit. I want you so bad," she begged.

Never one to disappoint his woman, he wrapped his lips around her swollen bud and sucked hard. She cried out, her entire body rocking against his face, as he sucked harder and harder until he felt her come undone. She screamed loudly, drenched in sweat, chest heaving as wave after wave of intense ecstasy consumed her entire body. He slid up her body, kissing her hard as he entered her.

She gasped at the power of his thrusts, never tiring of taking his entire length deep inside her body. He lovingly held her close as his dick moved in and out of her warm pussy, so wet from her orgasm, that his dick slid in and out with ease. She raked her nails down his back then grabbed his ass, trying to pull him in even deeper.

"I love you so much," he declared as he emptied himself inside her.

Keeping his arms around her, he laid on his back, pulling her on top of him. He groaned as she ground her pussy against his dick, getting him hard again. Feeling his erection, she took him inside, sitting up straight so he had full view of her naked body. They spent the next several hours making love and celebrating their engagement, until they were both so exhausted they quickly drifted off to sleep.

Chapter Twenty-Three

"We're gonna have a blast, can't wait. Later," Hannah heard Mikael say when she came downstairs.

"Good morning, sleepyhead," Mikael teased.

"Good morning, sexy," she said, gazing at her brand new diamond.

"Do you want some breakfast?" he asked.

"I would love some French toast."

Mikael started getting breakfast ready while Hannah got the coffee ready.

"Dean called about New Year's Eve. There's a special Karaoke party at the club."

"Yay! I'm so excited. We need to do another duet!"

"Absolutely. And it will be formal, so I thought we could wear the same clothes we did on Christmas."

"Of course! They should be done at the cleaners today."

After they ate breakfast, Hannah went down to the shop to do some cleaning. She hadn't been there since before Christmas and wanted to do some straightening up after their holiday rush. When she got there, she noticed the building next door had a for sale sign in the window. She called Mikael when she got inside.

"So, when I pulled up this morning, I saw that the store next to mine's for sale. Got me thinking about possibly expanding."

"I think that would be awesome, and maybe you could add a music section where people could shop for vintage vinyl or something like that."

"I love that idea. I need to get to work now. I'll grab lunch on my way home."

Mikael's wheels were already spinning when he said, "Sounds good."

After spending several hours getting everything done in the store and putting payroll through for Kurt and Amanda, she walked across the street to Garden of Eden to grab lunch. As she was walking back to her car, she noticed the sign had changed to sold. Damn, she thought to herself, I should have called right away. She hoped that whoever bought the store wouldn't cause her any problems. When she walked in, Mikael was sitting on the couch. When he saw the look on her face, he walked over and gave her a hug.

"What's wrong?"

"By the time I was done picking up lunch, the for sale sign was changed to a sold sign."

"I know."

Puzzled, Hannah asked, "How?"

"I bought it."

"I don't understand."

"I wanted to invest in your expansion, so I called the real estate agent and offered to pay in full. They jumped on the offer."

"Oh my god, thank you so much."

"We have an appointment later this afternoon to take care of all the paperwork. Let's eat quick then I need to go to the bank before our appointment."

Hannah threw her arms around his neck, "Thank you so much for this. I love you."

"I love you so much, baby."

"Can we go out and celebrate tonight?"

"You bet. How about we invite Dean and Alex, and Andy and Lizzie?"

"I would love that."

They scarfed down lunch then went upstairs to shower and change before heading out. Hannah was still in disbelief that someone would do something like this for her. She had very little experience with being treated this way, and she still sometimes had a fear that the rug was going to be pulled out from under her. Whenever she had those doubts, though, Mikael always did something to dispel them. She was so grateful he came into her life. Once they were ready, they headed to the bank first, then to the real estate office.

The real estate agent assigned to the property, John, took them to his office to sign the paperwork and complete the deal. Once he was done reviewing the details with Mikael, he handed him the papers to sign. Watching his hands work sent Hannah's mind to a naughty place. A jab in the side from Mikael's elbow snapped her back to reality.

"I'm adding your name to the deed, so you need to sign too," Mikael told Hannah.

She took the pen from him and signed the paperwork. Mikael had to stifle a laugh when he saw the color spreading across her cheeks. He could only imagine where her mind was when she wasn't responding to him. Once they finished at the real estate office, they headed home. Hannah called Alex and Lizzie and firmed up dinner plans. She and Mikael went upstairs to change into more casual clothes. Mikael came out of the bathroom and saw Hannah in jeans and a v-neck yellow t-shirt.

"Dammit woman, how are we going to make it to dinner?"

"Whatever do you mean?"

"You know that yellow drives me crazy."

"Damn right I know. Why else would I have picked this shirt?"

"So that's how we're playing!"

Mikael went back into his closet and shut the door. When he came out, he was wearing black leather pants and black button-down shirt. He left several buttons open, showing off his chest hair. When he opened the door and walked out, Hannah's jaw dropped.

"Holy shit," Hannah exclaimed.

"Two can play the dirty game, baby."

"We may need a trip to the restroom during dinner," she teased.

"We might!"

The group met at Hannah's favorite pizza place around six. They ordered four pies and a couple pitchers of beer for the table. Once the waiter had brought the beer, Mikael poured everyone a glass then stood.

"Hannah and I bought the building next to her shop today, so she can expand her store. Plus we're adding a vintage vinyl section that I'll help run," Mikael announced.

Dean and Alex offered to help in any way they could with getting things ready. Andy and Lizzie wished they could help, but had to get back to LA a couple days after New Year's. Andy seemed a little down about not being there, but he didn't say anything. When they were done dinner, they all met at Mikael and Hannah's house. The women stayed in the kitchen for some girl talk, which meant comparing bedroom tales, while the guys put on the Sixers game.

"Andy seems a little down today, everything okay?" Hannah asked Lizzie.

"There's been a little trouble in Dark Horse," Lizzie whispered.

"Oh no, I hope they can work it out. We're here if you ever need an ear," Alex added.

"Thanks, girls. But let's focus on good stuff."

After several steamy stories, the girls were all worked up.

"I think we're going to need to our men to service us tonight," Alex said.

"Yeah, but how are we going to pull them away from sports?" Hannah asked.

"Watch," Alex responded.

Alex stood behind Dean and ran her fingers through his hair. She whispered something in his ear and he flew off the couch.

"We gotta go," Dean exclaimed as they ran for the door.

Lizzie followed suit and the next thing Hannah and Mikael knew, they were alone. She sat down in Mikael's lap and showered his face and neck with kisses. He was trying to pay attention to the game but that battle was futile.

Without a word, she got up and walked upstairs. A few minutes later, she came back downstairs and Mikael damn near passed out cold. Hannah stood in front of him, hands on her hips. She was wearing a black lace bra, black crotchless panties that also showed off her bottom, and red suspenders. She finished the outfit with a firefighter's helmet. Mikael just sat there staring at her, mouth hanging open.

"I understand there's a very hot man that needs his flame extinguished," she purred.

Mikael's brain short-circuited and no words could make their way out of his mouth. He just kept sitting there staring at her. She leaned in, giving him a closeup view of her cleavage as she unbuttoned his shirt. She opened his shirt and showered his chest with kisses. She could feel his heart racing as she teased each of his nipples with her tongue. He just sat there, tongue hanging out, panting like a dirty dog while his sexy firefighter worked her magic on him. She pressed her chest into his, and the combination of lace and her warm skin was too much. He grabbed the remote and turned off the TV.

"Let's continue this upstairs," he begged.

She headed upstairs and could feel his eyes on her half-naked ass the whole way. When they were in their bedroom, she stood behind Mikael and ran her hands all over his naked chest. Fuck, she loved that sexy chest. After removing his shoes and socks, she went to work on his pants. First, though, she teased him, running her hand over his crotch, feeling how hard his cock was. She removed his belt, then opened the button and zipper. Sliding her hand inside his pants, she stroked his cock, making him growl. She finished removing his clothes and just stood there, her eyes absorbing every beautiful inch of his skin.

"On your back now," she commanded.

He laid down, licking his lips as he watched her crawl across the bed to him. Staying on all fours, she wrapped her hot lips around his dick, sucking hard, stopping with each stroke to run her tongue around the head. Fuck, she was do damn good at that. She angled her body so he could reach her pussy. He rubbed her clit while she sucked, her moans adding to the sensations on his cock until he was close to coming.

"Oh fuck, baby, I'm about to explode."

She sucked harder, gently squeezing his balls until he couldn't hold back, filling her beautiful mouth with his cum. She swallowed every last drop, then took her tongue and cleaned the rest of his delicious cream off his dick. He sat up and removed her suspenders, and bra, but left the panties on. He laid her on her back and spread he legs wide. Using a couple fingers to spread her folds, he slid his tongue into her pussy, licking up her sweet honey. When his tongue hit her clit, she lifted her hips off the bed, writhing in pleasure. He licked her slowly, pausing between each swipe.

"Please, don't stop, fuck, my pussy's aching for you."

He continued his slow torture, loving watching her desperate for him to lick her harder. He slowly increased his pressure and pace, her legs on his shoulders as she ran her fingers through his long hair. He slid his fingers inside her and after a few hard strokes, she came undone, quaking from head to toe as her orgasm coursed through her. He slid his body up hers, kissing her hard, tasting themselves on each other's tongues. Without breaking the kiss, he rolled onto his back, pulling her on top of him.

She grabbed his dick and slid it with ease into her pussy, still slick from her orgasm. Sitting up straight, giving Mikael full view of her sexy body, she bounced up and down his dick, hard and fast, both of them screaming loudly. Their bodies fit together perfectly, as if they were made for each other. He couldn't take his eyes of her tits bouncing as she fucked him. He reached around and squeezed her sexy ass.

"I've been a naughty girl tonight," she purred. "What are you going to do about it?"

She felt his hand lightly connect with her ass.

"I've been way naughtier than that."

He stroked her a little harder that time.

"Fuck, yes, like that, don't stop."

The sweet sting of his hands on her ass while his dick was so deep inside her felt so fucking good that she came hard. She squirted, drenching his cock, screaming as wave after wave of extreme ecstasy sent her into orbit. Keeping his dick inside her, he rolled her onto her back. He fucked her pussy hard, quickly emptying himself as he moved inside her. He collapsed next her, both of them drenched in sweat, chests heaving. He slid her panties off for her, then they grabbed a quick shower to clean up before heading back to bed. Mikael pulled the covers over their naked bodies and turned off the light.

"I really liked that outfit, baby."

"Really? I couldn't tell," she joked. That earned her one more light smack on her bare ass before they both drifted off to sleep.

The next day, they headed down to the shop to start looking at how they wanted to handle the expansion. They also checked out the new building. Hannah was starting to envision what it would like and she loved it already. When they were done checking everything out they walked over to Garden of Eden for lunch. A few minutes after Hannah and Mikael sat down, Eden came over to take their order and squealed when she saw Hannah's engagement ring.

"Wow, congratulations to you both. When did you get engaged?"

"Christmas Day," Hannah responded.

"I'm so happy for you both," she said, a sadness clouding her face.

'Thank you so much."

They spent the next couple of days doing some work on the store, getting ready for the construction. Before she knew it, it was finally New Year's Eve and Hannah was beyond excited for tonight's celebration. Once they were dressed and ready, they headed out. Alex made arrangements with her friends George and Margie to take care of all the pets while they were out. Mikael rented a limo so they could ride in style and not have to worry about driving.

The limo dropped them off at the performers' entrance, where Doug escorted them to their VIP table down front. Doug took their drink and food order personally. It sure was nice having connections like Dean and Alex, Hannah laughed to herself. Their waiter brought their drinks over and returned a little while later with their dinner. The group decided on ordering a bunch of appetizers to share. They ate and drank, awaiting Karaoke to start. Hannah and Mikael were planning to sing Peggy Lee's version of Fever and even had a bit of a dance planned.

Hannah got excited and nervous when she saw Doug walk on stage. Like he always did when he saw her, he called her up to kick things off. Mikael followed her to the stage. Hannah selected the song and once the music started, she and Mikael started their sexy dance and equally sexy vocals. Mikael was especially thankful his pants were loose, as he watched his sexy fiancée shaking her hips. He could barely focus on the screen and was glad they had practiced the song at home several times.

When they were done, they were with a loud ovation and obnoxious catcalls from their friends.

As they walked off the stage, Hannah mouthed follow me to Mikael. Instead of heading back to their table, she beelined for the club dressing room, Mikael hot on her heels. They went inside, Mikael closing and locking the door behind him.

"That was so damn sexy," she said.

"I bet those panties are nice and wet," he responded.

"They would be if I was wearing any."

"Fuck, woman," he growled.

Mikael walked over to the desk and bent her over. He ran his hands up her legs, lifting her dress as he went, leaving her bare ass exposed. He spread her legs, hearing her gasp when she felt his fingers massaging her pussy. He opened his pants and let them fall around his ankles, followed by his underwear. He stood behind her, sliding his dick deep into her pussy from behind. He fucked her hard and fast. They were so riled up from their performance that they came undone quickly. After another slap on her sexy ass, he grabbed a couple tissues for a quick cleanup. Once they had their clothes back in place, started to head back to the table.

"I'll meet you there, I need to hit the ladies' room," Hannah announced.

"Okay, my sexy woman."

Mikael walked back to the table. Hannah was about to enter the restroom when she heard a familiar voice.

"Talk about embarrassing."

"Mom, what are you doing here?"

"I came for what I thought would be a fun night out, and instead I get to be mortified by my fat daughter."

Everything Mikael had worked so hard to undo came rushing back. Hannah couldn't bear to face him. She knew he would be disgusted, so she ran out the back door. She ran past their limo and stopped when she got to the back of the parking lot, then sat down on the curb, head buried in her hands. She was so lost in thought, she never heard anyone approach and jumped when she felt an arm around her shoulder.

"Are you okay?" Kurt asked.

"Fine."

"Forgive me, but you don't look fine."

"I am, I promise. You should head inside. There's quite a party going on."

"You shouldn't be out here alone."

"Thanks, but I can take care of my own damn self. I always have."

Without saying another word, Kurt stood and walked toward the club. Hannah watched him walk away and felt bad at how she spoke to him when he was only trying to help. Typical for a worthless woman like you, she heard her mom's voice say.

When Kurt got inside, he saw Mikael and the others looking concerned, so he walked over.

"Sorry to interrupt, but when I got here, I saw Hannah sitting on the curb crying," Kurt told Mikael.

Mikael stood and held out his hand, "Thanks, Kurt."

Mikael headed outside until he found Hannah. He sat down next to her and wrapped her in his arms.

"What happened, baby.?"

"As I was heading into the restroom, I ran into my mom. She reminded me what a worthless woman I was. I couldn't bare to face you, so I took off. She reminded me that men don't want women like me."

"Forgive me for what I'm about to say, but your mother is a bitch. You're the sexiest woman I've ever known. You were so damn hot up on that stage, I'm surprised it didn't go up in flames."

Seeing the faintest hint of a smile appear on her beautiful face, Mikael continued, "Not to mention how incredible your voice is. Now, I need you to do something for me."

"What?"

"Stand up."

"And then," she said as she got to her feet.

"As loud as you can, tell your mom to fuck off."

"I can't."

"Yes you damn well can. You're a warrior-woman, so let me here you roar."

Hannah giggled then took a deep breath. "FUCK YOU, MOM," she screamed as a huge smile filled her face.

Bowing down to her, Mikael said, "Now, let's get back inside, hit that dance floor and show everyone my fierce woman, Sugartits!"

Laughing, she replied, "Okay, Pepperballs. Can we go in the back door, though?"

"Sure."

When they got back inside, Hannah stopped outside the ladies room. "Can you send Alex before I return to the table?"

"You bet. What should I tell the others?"

"You can tell them what happened."

"Okay. I love you," he said and kissed her forehead.

"I love you too."

Hannah walked inside the ladies room and was joined by Alex a few minutes later.

"Mikael told me what happened. What can I do?"

"I'm fine now, just need your help touching up my makeup before I go back out."

They headed back to the table once Alex finished working her magic. It was only a few minutes until midnight, so the three couples walked out to the dance floor. Waiters came around and handed everyone a glass of champagne. Mikael wrapped his arms around Hannah, holding her tight. The TVs were all showing the countdown to the ball drop in Times Square. Once the countdown began on the broadcast, everyone at the club joined in. When Mikael heard Ryan Seacrest yell Happy New Year, he crushed his lips to Hannah's, kissing her with more passion than she'd ever felt, Dean and Andy following his lead with Alex and Lizzie.

They all embraced in a circle afterwards, clinking glasses and downing their delicious champagne. Mikael kissed Hannah again, loving the taste of the champagne on her lips and tongue. He felt his dick starting to stir and had to talk himself down. Wait until I get that woman home, he thought to himself. I'll make sure she never doubts herself again. Once the party was over, they headed out to the limo.

Mikael and Hannah were the first dropped off. They practically ran out of the car, the rest of the group laughing at their urgency. Mikael heard cheers when he picked Hannah up and draped her over his shoulder. He waved before walking into the house. He put her down and pulled her close.

"Baby, you're the most beautiful woman I've ever known. Please, never doubt how damn sexy you are. You drive me wild, especially when your naked body's in my arms. And now, I'm taking you upstairs and spend the rest of the night proving that to you."

"I can't say thank you enough for what you've done for me. I love you."

"You don't have to thank me. Just get that hot ass up those stairs before my dick rips a hole in my pants."

She kicked her heels off and took off up the stairs, her sexy man in hot pursuit. The next day, they had to go out and buy a new bed!

CHAPTER 24

Epilogue

I n the months leading up to the wedding, Hannah and Mikael, along with several contractors and their friends, completed the work on the new store in between making wedding plans. Her co-matrons of honor, Alex and Lizzie, were amazing, as were Dean and Andy acting as co-best men for Mikael. The six of them had one hell of a pre-wedding bash in the Penthouse suite at Live! Casino and Hotel in Philadelphia. Unlike the characters in one of Hannah's favorite movies, The Hangover, they remembered what happened at their party!

Hannah and Mikael got married the first week of June in a beautiful outdoor ceremony at Eshelman Garden at the Lancaster Country Club. Hannah asked Kurt to walk her down the aisle. She was truly a vision in her cream-colored gown and bouquet of yellow daisies. Mikael went weak in the knees when he saw her round the corner on Kurt's arm. After reciting standard vows, they each shared personal vows with each other, Hannah going first.

"Mikael, before you danced your way into my life, I thought no man would ever want me. As hard as I fought you, you never gave up on me. Your friendship, love, and passion have meant more to me than words could ever express. I love you more than I ever knew was possible and I will continue to love and cherish you for the rest of our days."

"Hannah, I knew you were amazing way before you did. I was

reborn when I met you. I had become a mere shell of my former self. You reminded me how amazing and incredible loving a woman could be. You're my best friend, my lover and now, my wife. I will love and cherish you for the rest of our days."

"For the first time in public, it's my honor to present Mikael and Hannah Alfredsson."

Holding hands, Hannah and Mikael walked down the aisle to the applause of their guests, followed by Dean and Alex then Andy and Lizzie. Their reception lasted until the wee hours of the morning. The Monday following the wedding, the happy couple left for a blissful two-week honeymoon in Aruba, most of which they spent naked in bed.

Hannah also closed the shop and the stand during that time, giving Kurt and Amanda some well-earned time off. When they returned, Mikael started the hiring process for some to help run the record store part of their new store. One of the applicants was a guy named Johnny and he had been in a band in his younger days, playing drums. He had to walk away from music, citing personal reasons, but provided no details.

One afternoon, Hannah and Johnny were the only ones left in the store, and got to chatting.

"What brought you to Lancaster?" Hannah asked.

"Some things that happened in my life drove me here."

"Did you live here previously? Since the first time I saw you, something felt familiar about you."

"I did for a very short time as a very young child, but I have no real memories, just pictures."

"If I'm not prying, what was it specifically that made you move here?"

"I came to town after my father passed away. His death left me with no family, at least until I was given an envelope from his lawyer upon his death," Johnny lamented.

"I'm so sorry. Unfortunately, I completely understand. My father also recently passed away," Hannah replied.

"I'm so sorry."

"Thank you. So, this letter told you that you actually do have family?" Hannah asked.

"Yes, so I came to town to find her."

"Wow. What's her name? I may know her or be able to help?"

"Thank you for the offer, but I've actually found her."

"Wow, how exciting. What was finally meeting her like?"

"You tell me," he said.

"What do you mean?"

"I'm your twin brother."

About the Author

Samantha Michaels was born in 1973 in the small town of Abington, PA and was raised and still lives in Hatboro, PA (both suburbs of Philadelphia). She is married to her high school sweetheart and they have a rescue dog, a beautiful Black Lab named Holly.

When she's not writing or working at her full-time job, she enjoys watching her Philly sports team (hopefully) win, listening to heavy metal/hard rock music, reading, and spending time with friends and family.

Her love of reading began at a young age, thanks to her mother and Sesame Street. Her mom read to her constantly, and by three years old, she was reading on her own, and hasn't stopped. This eventually turned into a love of writing. She was writing for herself and then for a small group of friends, one of whom told her she should be writing books. She took her friends advice and has since published several romance books with plenty more on the way.

Also by Samantha Michaels

The Rockstar Quadrilogy

Leather and Lace

A Second Shot at Love

Pet Shop Passion

Silent Angel - Coming April 2022

The Melody of the Seasons

Rockin' Spring

Rockin' Summer

Rockin' Autumn - Coming September 2022

Rockin' Winter - Coming December 2022

www.ingramcontent.com/pod-product-compliance
Lightning Source LLC
Chambersburg PA
CBHW020633180626
46816CB00003B/936